Text and illustrations copyright © 2023 by Jane Cabrera
All Rights Reserved
HOLIDAY HOUSE is registered in the U.S. Patent and Trademark Office.
Printed and bound in November 2022 at C&C Offset, Shenzhen, China.
www.holidayhouse.com
First Edition
1 3 5 7 9 10 8 6 4 2

Library of Congress Cataloging-in-Publication Data

Names: Cabrera, Jane, author, illustrator.
Title: The Daily Sniff / Jane Cabrera.
Description: First edition. | New York : Holiday House, [2023] | Audience:
Ages 4-8. | Audience: Grades K-1. | Summary: "Ted, a dog who gets his
news each day by smelling out The Daily Sniff, investigates when his
town is overcome by an unusual odor, which turns out to be a skunk
family"— Provided by publisher.
Identifiers: LCCN 2021043621 | ISBN 9780823452316 (hardcover)
Subjects: CYAC: Dogs—Fiction. | Skunks—Fiction. | Smell—Fiction.
LCGFT: Picture books.
Classification: LCC PZ7.C1135 Dai 2023 | DDC [E]—dc23
LC record available at https://lccn.loc.gov/2021043621

ISBN: 978-0-8234-5231-6 (hardcover)

THE DAILY SNIFF

Jane Cabrera

HOLIDAY HOUSE · NEW YORK

Ted was a dog who liked to keep up
with all the latest news.

But did you know that dogs get their news
through The Daily Sniff?
Each and every day they sniff around town . . .

to get local news

and news from far away too.

But one day, poor Ted had to stay in.
He missed The Daily Sniff, and
he did not like the cone. Not one little bit.

His family tried to cheer him up.

At long last, the day came when Ted could go out again and catch up on The Daily Sniff.
But he could smell no news. No news at all.

Instead, there was just a really bad smell all over town.
Ted set off to investigate.
Was it the supermarket's dumpster?

Was it the fish market?

Was it the cows at the edge of town?
No, it was none of these,
although they were all rather smelly too.

Ted sniffed all over town with no luck.
So he gave up and went home.

But home did not smell right.
Inside the garage, Dad's hat
was moving by itself!

Underneath it was . . .

a skunk! "Help!" said the skunk.

"I cannot find my five little brothers and sisters anywhere."
Of course, Ted wanted to help!

"Thank you, Ted,"
said the skunk.
Finally, all the baby skunks were
carried back home to the forest.

And The Daily Sniff soon returned,
with local news . . .

and with news from far away too.

ANNE BLANCHARD | EMMANUEL CERISIER

Arab Science and Invention in the Golden Age

Translated by R. M. BRENT

ENCHANTED LION BOOKS

New York

The author would like to thank Françoise Micheau, professor of medieval history of the Muslim world at the University of Paris I, for generously sharing her talents and knowledge.

The author also thanks Florence Langevin for her precious collaboration.

Author

Anne Blanchard got her start working as an editor, first in social studies, then in children's books. She now writes and develops articles and books on diverse subjects. One of her books, *The Big Book of Dummies, Rebels and Other Geniuses* has just been published by Enchanted Lion Books.

Illustrator

To create his accurate, detailed, and highly realistic illustrations, **Emmanuel Cerisier** is uncompromising with himself, his pencil, and his watercolors. He has published several books with Casterman.

Expert

Ahmed Djebbar is Professor of Mathematics and the History of Mathematics at the University of Science and Technology in Lille, France. His has written extensively on Muslim science and its golden age.

Translator

RM Brent began his translation career with Firelight Foundation (San Jose, California), which funds AIDS relief work in Africa. This is his first translation of a book.

Calligraphy : Lassaad Metoui
Editorial Conception: Bayard Éditions Jeunesse and Anne Blanchard / *Marque de Fabrique*
Artistic Direction: Studio Bayard Éditions Jeunesse
Graphic Conception: François Egret / *Amulette*
Documentary and Picture Research: Anne Silve and Nadège Cauchois for *Marque de Fabrique*

First American Edition published in 2008 by
Enchanted Lion Books, 201 Richards Street, Studio 4, Brooklyn, NY 11231

Originally published in French as *le Grand Livre des Sciences et Inventions Arabes*

Bayard Editions Jeunesse © 2006

Translation © 2008 Enchanted Lion Books

[A CIP record is on file with the Library of Congress]

ISBN-10: 1-59270-080-2
ISBN-13: 978-1-59270-080-6

Printed in China by South China Printing Co., Ltd.

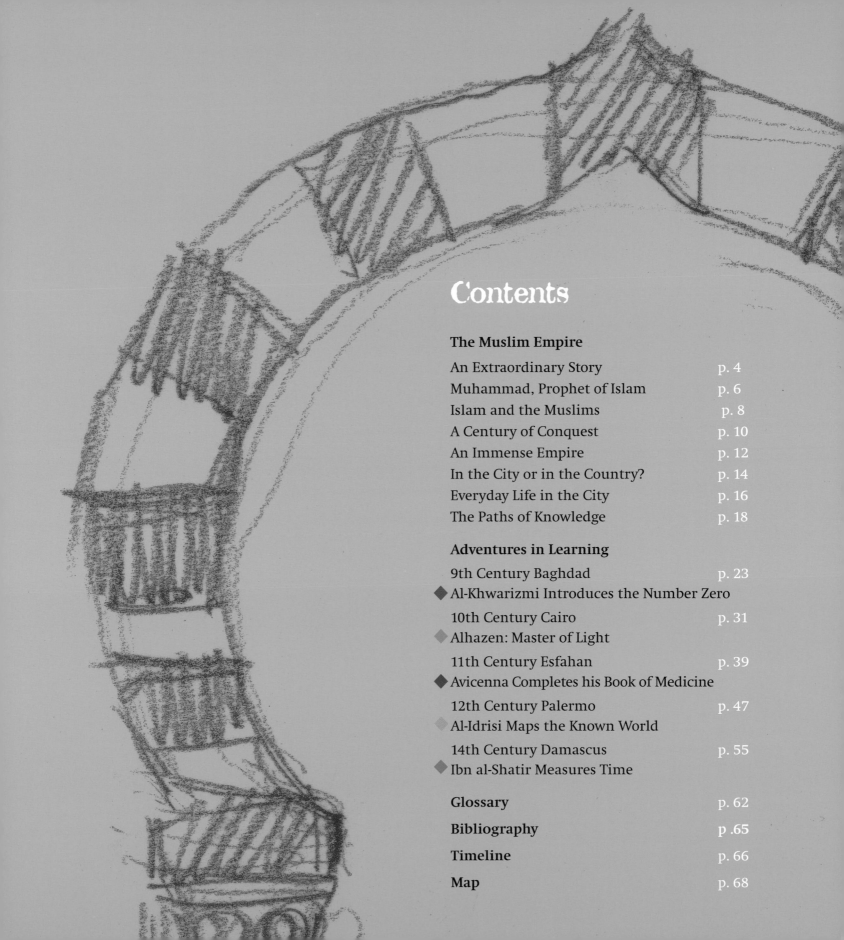

Contents

The Muslim Empire

Adventures in Learning

An extraordinary story

From the 8th to the 15th century, the Muslim Empire witnessed an amazing scientific adventure.

The Muslim world: once a single empire, now a multitude of countries

The current Muslim world encompasses fifty or so countries. However, in the world of yesterday—well, perhaps the day before yesterday, during an era that corresponded to the European Middle Ages—it formed an enormous empire.

It all began early in the 7th century when the prophet Muhammad and his first followers achieved a series of military victories, which allowed them to establish their religion, Islam (founded by Muhammad), and their language, Arabic, in the countries they had conquered.

The historical period covered in this book is considered insofar as it pertains to the Muslim Empire, which encompassed the following modern countries: (from east to west) Morocco, Mauritania, Algeria, Tunisia, Turkey, Libya, Egypt, Syria, Jordan, Lebanon, Israel, Iraq, Iran, and Afghanistan; (from north to south) Saudi Arabia, Yemen, and Oman.

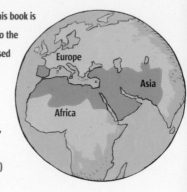

Arabic and Islam thus became common elements shared by nearly all of the inhabitants of a single territory that had expanded considerably in less than a century. Its borders reached as far as the kingdoms of India, the empires of China and Byzantium, as well as the West, which was itself divided into many kingdoms.

7th Century: The creation of the Muslim Empire

8th Century

Throughout the Middle Ages, Muslims shared borders with the rest of the world, most notably with the West. Here are some useful dates for understanding the interaction between the East and the West. Certain dates apply to both, whereas other dates are reference points for the 21st century reader.

THE EAST

THE WEST

For the Muslims, it was a great accomplishment that they were able to advance into European lands as far as the kingdom of France!

For inhabitants of the kingdom of France, the victory of Charles Martel over the Muslims at Poitiers in 732 was a source of great pride. Martel's success allowed him to regain the throne, enabling him to establish his descendants as his successors. (Pepin and Charlemagne belong to this line.)

For centuries, the Muslim world was ahead in science

The golden age of Muslim science began in the 8th century, impelled by the efforts of the empire's rulers, or caliphs. Every major city participated in and contributed to this period of scientific adventure and discovery. In schools, hospitals, and the salons of wealthy citizens, people discussed astronomy, mathematics, mechanics, and medicine.

Four hundred years later, in the 12th century, as cultural and scientific revolutions began to

occur throughout Europe, the scientific innovations of the Muslim world slowly came to an end. Interest in scientific discovery was eclipsed by crisis: first the Crusades, beginning at the end of the 11th century, and then the Mongol invasions of the 13th and 14th centuries. Wealthy merchant cities began to decline. Some, falling into ruin, were completely abandoned. By the 14th century, the age of Muslim science was over.

9th Century

Around the year 800, the West and the East exchanged ambassadors and gifts. Of note was Caliph Harun al-Rashid's presentation of a clock to Emperor Charlemagne.

11th to 13th Century

13th-14th Centuries: The Mongol Invasions

The Muslim world experienced the Crusades as a series of massacres and attacks perpetrated by Christian armies. The great Christian victories, achieved so far from home, can be explained in part by the failure of the Muslim Empire's rulers to agree amongst themselves to unite their forces and drive back the enemy.

In European history, the Crusades—two hundred years of sieges and conquest in Muslim lands—are viewed as a pivotal event. They were motivated, in particular, by the importance the Christian kingdoms placed on the city of Jerusalem, which had been conquered by the Muslims

Muhammad,
Prophet of Islam

Little is known of Muhammad's life before the age of 40, when he began preaching a new religion called Islam.

Arabia: birthplace of Muhammad

The dromedary can travel over 30 miles without water and is able to carry up to 90 pounds of goods or supplies on its back.

Arabia was a vast territory of great geographic diversity. Its coast on the Indian Ocean received rainfall from the monsoons, and its fertile fields were envied by its neighbors. To the north, however, was an immense desert traversed by nomads, who subsisted through raising sheep, goats, and dromedaries.

The Arabian Desert gives way to mountains, and beyond the summits of these mountains lies the Red Sea. At the foot of these mountains on the desert side, a caravan route linked prosperous cities such as Medina and Mecca.

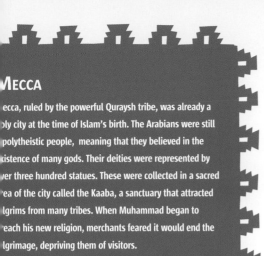

Mecca

Mecca, ruled by the powerful Quraysh tribe, was already a holy city at the time of Islam's birth. The Arabians were still a polytheistic people, meaning that they believed in the existence of many gods. Their deities were represented by over three hundred statues. These were collected in a sacred area of the city called the Kaaba, a sanctuary that attracted pilgrims from many tribes. When Muhammad began to preach his new religion, merchants feared it would end the pilgrimage, depriving them of visitors.

Muhammad's life before forty

Muhammad was born in Mecca in the year 570, into the Quraysh tribe. Raised by his uncle, Abu Talib, a caravan merchant and a leading citizen of the city, Muhammad spent his childhood traveling all over Arabia at his uncle's side. As a young man, he was hired to take care of the caravans belonging to a widow named Khadidja, who later became his wife.

As the leader of a caravan, Muhammad probably made at least two trips a year: one in winter, and one in summer. Upon returning from his travels, his custom was to sleep alone in a cave on Mount Hira, part of the mountain range that surrounds Mecca. As he later recounted, it was there, around the year 610, that he heard the voice of the angel Gabriel for the first time.

Revelations of the Prophet

Little by little, Gabriel revealed to Muhammad the nature of God and his advice for humankind. With the help of his wife, his 10-year-old cousin Ali, and his friend Abu Bakr, Muhammad spread the divine word throughout the city of Mecca. Its inhabitants, however, had no desire to abandon their beliefs, and his preaching was given a hostile, even mocking, reception.

From exile to power

Persecuted, Muhammad left in 622 for the oasis town of Yathrib, which soon would be renamed Medina, meaning "city of the Prophet." There he united different tribes around the concepts of fraternity, mutuality, and solidarity. Eight years later, having become a true military and political leader, he won a series of battles against his opponents.

When he returned victorious to his native city of Mecca, Muhammad emptied the Kaaba sanctuary of its ancient gods. He then gathered Arabians from both the north and the south behind him, converting them to Islam. By the time of his death in 632, he had become the powerful leader of the Muslims, an Islamic community that had already begun to resemble a small country.

THE MUSLIM CALENDAR

Unlike the Christian calendar, the Muslim calendar begins with the Prophet's exile and exodus from Mecca, which corresponds to the year 622 when referenced to the calendar used today. The date of Muhammad's exile (called the Hegira) marks year 1 of the Muslim calendar.

The angel Gabriel

7

Islam and the Muslims

The Koran is the sacred book of the Muslims. Since Muhammad did not write, but preached, his teachings were collected and written down after his death.

The Koran: first spoken...

The Koran is the word of God, spoken to the Prophet Muhammad through the voice of the angel Gabriel. It did not first appear as a book; indeed, the word Koran itself means "the recitation." This is fitting since according to Muhammad, he merely recited the words dictated to him by the angel Gabriel. At the time, writing was not common. Rather, people learned through memorization, as Muhammad's first followers did.

...then written

To combat the ancient gods and beliefs, the need grew for a book upon whose text the Muslims could rely. This book would allow all Muslims to practice their religion together and in the same manner. Upon Muhammad's death in 632, the first Muslim caliphs ordered the Koran to be written down. Undoubtedly carried out by a group of highly learned men, the writing of the Koran took many, many years.

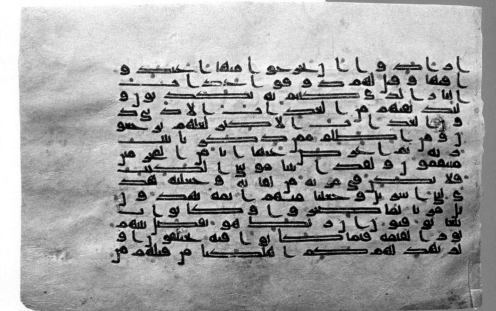

Scribes reproduced the Koran using sharpened reed straws to write. Their ink was made from a base of charred sheep's wool.

WRITING WITHOUT PAPER

In Arabia, palm leaves, flat stones, and the shoulder blades of camels were used to write on. In Egypt, writing was done on papyrus, which grew all along the Nile, and on parchment made from animal hides. Gazelle hide was chosen for recording the Koran, because it is thin and supple. Books remained extremely rare up until the 8th century, when the Muslims learned to produce paper.

MUHAMMAD, LAST OF THE PROPHETS

For Muslims, Muhammad is the last in a line of prophets through whom God communicated with human beings. Adherents of Islam also recognize the importance of Moses, the Jewish prophet, and of Jesus, the prophet of Christianity. However, according to Islam, the divine message imparted by Moses and Jesus through the books of the Torah and the Bible has been distorted. For Muslims, Muhammad stands as the last prophet of all time, and the one true messenger of God, called "Allah" in Arabic.

The Suras, written in the sacred language of Arabic

Arabic, in which the 114 chapters, or suras, of the Koran were written, became the language of prayer for all Muslims. The Koran does not constitute a single text; it is a book composed of many diverse writings: prayers, hymns, life lessons, stories, and more. According to religious scholars, the "inimitable beauty" of the Koran is the reflection of God Himself.

Who is God? Muhammad receives the revelations of the angel Gabriel

There exists but one all-merciful God, who is the Creator of the universe. The very proof of divine goodness lies in the creation of sky, earth, the order of the world, and man and woman, who emerged from dust. In return, human beings owe God their gratitude and submission. Reborn in the hereafter, human beings either attain Paradise or descend to Hell, depending on their actions in life.

As in all religions, not all believers take the Revelation literally; many interpret it in symbolic terms.

Friday prayer is the primary reason for attending mosque. Mosques also have libraries where the faithful can consult books that they otherwise might be unable to obtain. Finally, the mosque serves as a place for relaxation and meditation, as well as political gatherings.

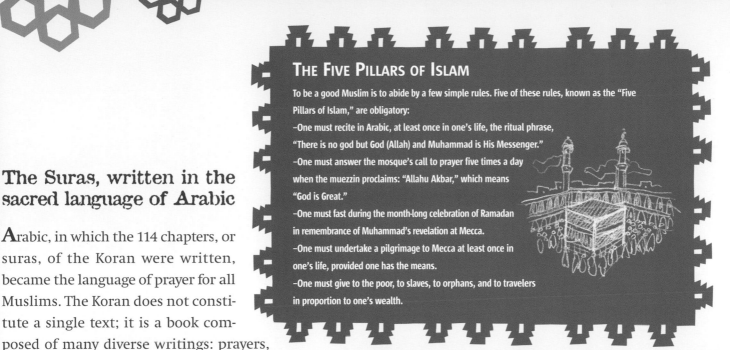

THE FIVE PILLARS OF ISLAM

To be a good Muslim is to abide by a few simple rules. Five of these rules, known as the "Five Pillars of Islam," are obligatory:

–One must recite in Arabic, at least once in one's life, the ritual phrase, "There is no god but God (Allah) and Muhammad is His Messenger."

–One must answer the mosque's call to prayer five times a day when the muezzin proclaims: "Allahu Akbar," which means "God is Great."

–One must fast during the month-long celebration of Ramadan in remembrance of Muhammad's revelation at Mecca.

–One must undertake a pilgrimage to Mecca at least once in one's life, provided one has the means.

–One must give to the poor, to slaves, to orphans, and to travelers in proportion to one's wealth.

A century of conquest

Within about a hundred years, the Arabian tribes had conquered a territory that extended from Spain to the borders of India and China.

Not enough land for so many rulers

From the time of Medina onward, Muhammad's closest associates exercised power one after another, taking the title of caliph following his death in 632. Muhammad's successors included his friend, Abu Bakr, and his cousin, Ali. However, each time a caliph died, the choice of a successor unleashed conflict. The solution that was found was to expand the Prophet's territories in order to give each candidate an opportunity to realize his ambitions. This solution also allowed for the spread of Muhammad's teachings, which was of profound importance. Thus it was that the Muslims set off to conquer new lands.

MUSLIM CONQUEST IN EUROPE

Spain was under Muslim rule from the 8th century until the Christian kingdoms recaptured it beginning in the 11th century. It was not until the 15th century, however, that Muslim Spain completely disappeared, following the fall of Grenada in 1492. Traces, of course, remain. For example, Andalusia, a southern region of present-day Spain, took its name from the Arabic: al-Andalus.

Muslims also ruled the island of Sicily (now part of Italy) from the 10th - 11th century, before its recapture by Christian forces.

Horsemen on a mission

The Arabian forces were lead by keen and committed commanders. The soldiers, mostly Muslim, were probably inspired in their fight against infidels (non-Muslims) by a verse from the Koran, which incites believers to, "Fight in the path of God." Their enthusiasm paid off, and they successfully defeated the already-weakened armies of the great Persian and Byzantine Empires.

In the 7th and 8th centuries, they seized the territories of present-day Syria, the city of Jerusalem, and, finally, Egypt and Armenia. The Persian Empire crumbled when Muslim horsemen conquered present-day Iraq and Iran.

Populations capitulate and convert to Islam

These initial victories must have greatly encouraged the conquerors. Once the chaos of battle had passed, the populations accepted their new rulers. Daily life was not particularly affected, as the Muslims allowed Christians, Jews, and pagans (whose numbers remained substantial) to continue to practice their religion on the condition that they pay a special tax.

Some inhabitants of the conquered lands converted to Islam, either from belief or self-interest, and some even became soldiers, choosing the path of conquest for themselves. As a result of this reinforcement, the original Arabian forces were transformed into a powerful Muslim army.

Several thousand warriors were quickly joined by new fighters.

At China's doorstep

In the 8th century, the Muslims continued eastward until they reached the border of China. They were prudent, however; realizing how far they had traveled from home, their commanders chose to pull back in order to focus on the territory already acquired, where order and calm had yet to be established.

Their forces advanced northward as well, but were unable to overcome the empire of Byzantium (this included present-day Turkey), which would remain a powerful adversary for centuries to come.

Checked in Europe

The Muslim army continued its advance through the Maghreb. After capturing Egypt, it gained control of the territories of present-day Libya, Tunisia, Algeria, and Morocco.

Are these grenades or humble beer bottles? Historians do not really know how these receptacles were used.

Once there, the Muslims were separated from the West by only the ten short miles of the Straight of Gibraltar, which they successfully crossed to occupy Spain. Passing over the Pyrenees, they next advanced on the territory of present-day France. Muslim forces, however, were rebuffed at Poitiers in 732 by the forces of Charles Martel, the great-grandfather of the future emperor of the West, Charlemagne. Nevertheless, the Muslims remained in the south of France until the 9th century, when they withdrew to Spain and Portugal.

An immense empire

It was not easy to govern such a vast territory, and different regions quickly began to compete for power, which was divided among various factions. What maintained the Muslim Empire's true unity was Arabic, its common language.

A unified empire, inclusive of its native populations

The Muslim Empire was very powerful, and most of its inhabitants were linked by a single religion, which, despite having diverged into several branches, remained a unifying force. Above all, however, it was their ability to speak and understand Arabic that unified them more than anything else. This was exceptional for such a vast territory, and it was the driving force behind the empire's power. Throughout their conquests, the Muslims were also enriched by their discoveries, which proved to be another significant asset. For example, their armies became more effective by adopting the weapons and tactics of their adversaries, such as crossbows and grenades.

The empire weakens

Throughout the 12th and 13th centuries, the Muslim Empire was the target of the Crusades. The result was that Mediterranean trade, which guaranteed a large portion of the empire's wealth, passed from Muslim control to Western merchants.

In the second half of the 13th century, a new danger threatened the Muslim Empire: the invasion of the Mongols. Its forces ravaged all that stood in their path. They invaded Baghdad and assassinated the caliph. With that, the Muslim Empire, already severely weakened by rivalries between its rulers, ceased to exist.

Sana'a (in present-day Yemen)

Cordoba
(in present-day Spain).

The Capital of the Muslim Empire

Although Mecca remained the destination of the great Muslim pilgrimage, it did not stay at the center of the empire for long. The Umayyads, a branch of the Prophet's family, took power around the middle of the 7th century, and established their capital at Damascus (in present-day Syria). A century later, almost all of the members of this dynasty had been killed by another branch of the Prophet's family, the Abbassids, who founded the new city of Baghdad, which they designated as the capital of the empire.

Some cities continued their resistance for several decades, while others, such as Cairo, succeeded in driving out the Mongols altogether. It was the beginning of a new era in which there never again would be just one territorial empire that all Muslims called home.

Rival Caliphs

The caliph of Baghdad was strongly challenged: on one hand, he was rebelled against; on the other, rulers elsewhere in the empire also laid claim to the title of caliph. This situation resulted in the creation of two competing caliphates: one in Andalusia, beginning in the 8th century, in the city of Cordoba in Muslim Spain; and another in Cairo, Egypt, in the 9th century. By the 11th century, the caliph of Baghdad was so weakened that Turkish soldiers, who controlled the empire's military, were able to seize power. Nevertheless, the caliph of Baghdad continued to exert his influence as the spiritual leader of all Muslims, and most of the rulers governing the different regions of the empire continued to recognize his authority up through the 13th century.

In the city or in the country?

There were many more peasants than city dwellers in the Muslim Empire. Nevertheless, it was in its cities that its true wealth and splendor were on display.

In the cities, power and wealth...

Thanks to the spoils of conquest, the victors were able to build cities surrounded by high fortifications and to expand the encampments of their soldiers. These fortified cities allowed them to assert control over their territory.

At the center of these cities, inside the palaces, caliphs, viziers, and emirs surrounded themselves with influential people, such as wealthy landowners, judges, and high-ranking imperial bureaucrats. During an imperial audience or a major festival, the palace doors were also open to the richest inhabitants of the city, its merchants.

... attracted new residents...

The city streets teemed with the life brought by the new motley population of diverse origins and religions. Townspeople, peasants, soldiers, servants, and beggars, as well as many Christians and Jews, all lived side by side.

Baghdad, founded in the 8th century, had a population of over a million inhabitants by the 10th century—more than twenty times the popula-

Urban homes usually were made of brick, and their walls were covered with thatch.

tion of Paris at the time! Cordoba and Cairo were both home to hundreds of thousands of people. These large populations, always quick to revolt against the current establishment, were a threat to the emirs and the caliphs.

...who were fed by the countryside...

To ensure calm among the people, it was essential for everyone to have enough to eat. This was not always the case, however, even though the large cities of Damascus, Baghdad, Fes, and Cairo were situated near an oasis or an agricultural

The rich interior of a Persian house.

region. Wisely, the caliph decided to set aside reserve provisions for the city, which he sold back at reduced prices during times of famine. Moreover, merchants were forbidden to increase their wealth by speculating on the price of food.

...and prospered through trade

Merchant caravans traversed the empire, traveling through Asia and Africa, loaded with valuable and highly sought-after goods. They brought wood, a rare commodity in the Middle East, which lacked forests; spices; gold; and slaves. Merchants sometimes ran shops in several different souks.

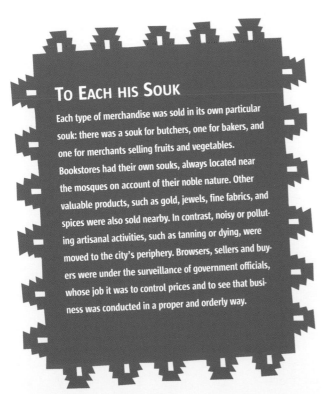

TO EACH HIS SOUK

Each type of merchandise was sold in its own particular souk: there was a souk for butchers, one for bakers, and one for merchants selling fruits and vegetables. Bookstores had their own souks, always located near the mosques on account of their noble nature. Other valuable products, such as gold, jewels, fine fabrics, and spices were also sold nearby. In contrast, noisy or polluting artisanal activities, such as tanning or dying, were moved to the city's periphery. Browsers, sellers and buyers were under the surveillance of government officials, whose job it was to control prices and to see that business was conducted in a proper and orderly way.

Everyday life
in the city

Throughout the day, activities were organized around prayer time, but also in regard to the temperature: the streets grew calm at the hottest time of the day, coming alive again at night.

Around the mosque

The different neighborhoods of the city were built around the caliph's palace, when there was one, and the grand mosque. On Friday at noon, many Muslims gathered at the mosque for prayer; this was also where men came to chat and boys to study. As the cities grew, the number of grand mosques increased, and by the end of the 10th century, Baghdad already had six!

Bathing and purification

Canals brought water to the mosque for ritual ablutions, and to the public baths, called hammams, which were located nearby. The Prophet recommended bathing twice a week for hygienic purposes, advice that was echoed by doctors. Since homes were not equipped for bathing, hammams were built all over the city. By the 10th century, Baghdad had one on every street!

Learning Arabic, the Koran, and arithmetic

While boys born into well-off families "went to school" from age 6 to 16, they really went to the homes of teachers, or to the mosque. All were taught Arabic, the Koran, and arithmetic. Girls born into privileged families also benefitted from an education, which was sometimes very advanced. Some of them became doctors, poets, or legal specialists. One woman held a literary salon in Baghdad in the 10th century. During the same century, a mathematician name Lubna lived in the court of the caliph of Cordoba. She served as secretary to the caliph, which was a very prestigious position.

The hammam, open to men in the morning and women in the afternoon, was an important place to meet and talk.

In the stories of the *One Thousand and One Nights*, flying carpets soar through the air. In reality, carpets were on the ground everywhere, tossed over floors of houses, in gardens, and even oases. A carpet defined a private space, and also served to mark out a space for prayer. When spread on a platform and covered with cushions, a rug became a gathering place.

From age 16, students attended madrasa

The strongest students went on to study at madrasas, which were financed by the caliph or by wealthy individuals. As they offered food and lodging, many students also lived there. Their education was free and encompassed various material related to Islam. Some madrasas, few in number, also taught literature, law, and science. Attending madrasa was the best way to become a grammarian, judge, or astronomer.

The study of theology at the city's great mosques was another path available to young Muslims.

NIGHTTIME RENDEZVOUS

In Arabic, the word "samar" means "to discuss at night." Once night had fallen, it was time for stories and for reading travel accounts. People gathered around the caliph, a poet, or a storyteller, and listened to the stories of the *One Thousand and One Nights*, which recounted the escapades of historical figures, such as the Caliph Harun al-Rashid, as well as the adventures of legendary heroes, such as Sinbad the sailor or Aladdin.

TWENTY-FIVE YEARS OF ADVENTURE!

Travelers, driven by a desire to see the world, voyaged from one end of the empire to another. Upon their return, they wrote down their adventures in books intended for wealthy city dwellers. The adventures of Ibn Battuta, for example, became very famous. He left Tangiers (present-day Morocco) at the age of 21, and did not return home until twenty-five years later. During that time, he made six pilgrimages to Mecca, married several times, and escaped from shipwrecks. He traveled beyond the limits of the empire, all the way into Russia, India, and China. He even worked as a judge on an island in the Indian Ocean. His adventures, whether in written or spoken form, delighted the urban populations.

The paths of knowledge

Throughout history, people have drawn upon the knowledge of their predecessors of all cultures to produce the scientific innovations that slowly but surely advance humanity; Muslims and Christians were no different.

Greek knowledge

The Greeks of classical antiquity were prosperous traders, whose civilization—standing at the crossroads of Africa, Asia and Europe—came to dominate the Mediterranean world. Their civilization reached its peak between 400 and 300 BCE. In Athens, political thought and democracy were born, and through the philosophy of Aristotle and the geography of Ptolemy, the Greeks advanced the revolutionary idea that humans, at the center of the universe, are in control of both themselves and the world. Additionally, the Greeks excelled in mathematics, geometry and medicine.

How did the Muslims discover Greek culture?

Eventually, the Greek Empire declined and was absorbed into the powerful Roman Empire. The scientific knowledge of the Greeks was lost, and their manuscripts lay forgotten on library shelves, not to be rediscovered for many centuries. In the meantime, the Roman Empire came to dominate a large portion of Europe, the Middle East, and the Mediterranean coast. By the 5th century CE, however, the Roman Empire itself began to crumble under pressure from the invasions from Central Europe. Only the eastern part, including the territory of present-day Turkey, survived. This eastern empire would endure for another thousand years.

The texts of Byzantium

The Eastern Roman Empire, later called the Byzantine Empire, or simply Byzantium, possessed hundreds of Greek manuscripts, in which a newfound interest slowly began to emerge. Muslims discovered these manuscripts following their victories in Byzantium, and became fascinated by them. Muslim scholars were also able to read books borrowed from the Byzantine emperor during times of peace. They translated them into Arabic and, drawing upon the knowledge they contained, they stimulated a new wave of scientific discovery.

European discovery

The wars of reclamation, waged by the Christians in Spain and Italy, and the Crusades, which began towards the end of the 11th century, brought Christians into contact with Muslims. European scholars heard that the Muslims had studied the Greek texts and were adept in the sciences. At the time, Europeans were thirsty for knowledge, for they had yet to build their great libraries or universities (these began to appear in the 12th century). Western scholars began to study the Arabic manuscripts and translated them into Latin, sometimes from a desire to learn, but also in an attempt to prove that Muslim culture was inferior to Christian culture. Yet, as the West rediscovered the ancient Greek texts through their Arabic translations, it also benefitted from Arab inventions and discoveries.

ARABIC, HEBREW, AND LATIN

To translate the texts from Arabic into Latin, Christians enlisted the help of many Jewish scholars, who had lived for years as subjects of the Muslim Empire, and would remain after the Christians took control. These Jewish scholars had already translated many manuscripts from Arabic into their own language, Hebrew. Since some also knew Latin, their collaboration was essential for the Christian translators.

In both Andalusia and the Pyrenees, monks translated the books written by Muslim scholars.

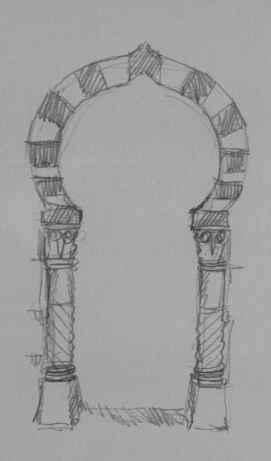

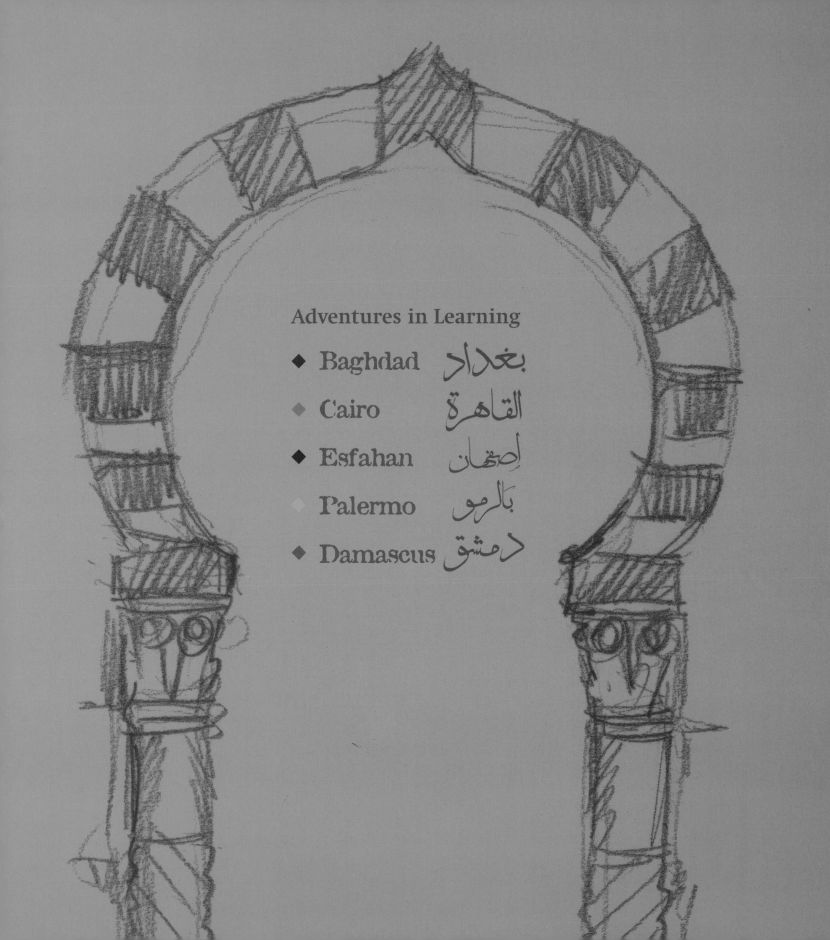

Adventures in Learning

- Baghdad بغداد
- Cairo القاهرة
- Esfahan اصفهان
- Palermo بالرمو
- Damascus دمشق

9th century Baghdad

Al-Khwarizmi introduces the number zero

Toward the middle of the 8th century, according to the wishes of the ruling caliphs, Iraq became the center of the Muslim Empire. This new capital would bear witness to the start of an amazing scientific revolution.

A city is built on the banks of the Tigris following the advice of astrologers

It is said that in the year 762, the Caliph al-Mansur summoned the greatest astrologers in the land to ask them where the best place to establish the capital of his empire would be. Thanks to numerous calculations, the stars spoke, indicating that the caliph had to build on one of the banks of the Tigris.

This was excellent advice since the Tigris and the Euphrates are the two major rivers that irrigate the region. The location identified by the astrologers was, thus, a point of intersection between many canals and trades routes of the empire.
The city rose up quickly, and the peasants of the surrounding countryside called it Baghdad, the name of a small village that already existed.

Baghdad attracts the riches of the world

Baghdad quickly prospered, and commercial districts began to surround the grand mosque and the palace of the caliph.

Merchandise arrived from the four corners of the empire as well as from elsewhere in the world, such as China, India, and Africa. Rare goods, such as spices, manuscripts, and precious gems, were highly prized by princes, powerful merchants, and dignitaries.
Hundreds of hammams opened their doors to the population as well as to visitors attracted by the most powerful city in the empire. A workshop also opened that specialized in embroidered fabrics that were bound for the court.
Less than twenty years after the city's founding, the first hospital was constructed on the order of Caliph Harun al-Rashid, al-Mansur's successor.

In Baghdad, paper pulp began to be manufactured beginning in the 8th century. The circulation of knowledge thus became easier thanks to manuscripts written or copied onto paper. As the story goes, the secret of making paper (far less expensive than parchment) was extracted from Chinese prisoners in exchange for their liberty. The city now had all the tools it needed to become a capital of literature, art, and science!

Baghdad, built on a perfectly circular plot, was protected by fortifications around which townships quickly sprang up. At the time, Baghdad was an enormous city, whereas cities in Europe, such as Venice and Paris, were sparsely populated by comparison.

Thanks to Arabic, Greek knowledge came out of obscurity

The scientific era that developed and flourished within the Muslim Empire throughout the Middle Ages began in Baghdad. One of its most important participants was Al-Khwarizmi.

Among the automatons created for the amusement of the princes and the richest in the city, a number of models served water or wine.

A house of wisdom

The scholars of Baghdad, as well as those from all over the empire, gathered at the House of Wisdom, which was founded under the reign of Caliph Harun al-Rashid. They worked in the library, where they met with students, and conducted seminars on science, philosophy, and religion. Assembling the greatest minds of the city together in one place was an excellent idea, and one that was soon imitated. Wealthy, educated patrons began to establish libraries and Houses of Science, smaller than the House of Wisdom, in other imperial cities.

Manuscripts from Byzantium

Al-Mamun, son of Harun al-Rashid, succeeded his father at the beginning of the 9th century. The new caliph was passionate about science, and sought to increase his knowledge and that of the city's scholars. To do this, he collected the manuscripts of Greece, Persia and India that were scattered throughout his empire. Some were over seven hundred years old. He also borrowed a portion of the library belonging to the emperor of Byzantium (modern-day Istanbul), and had every work of philosophy, mathematics, science, and literature that he found among its volumes copied.

A fortune spent on translations!

One problem remained, however: most of the texts were written in Greek! Now that they had been copied, they had to be translated into Arabic. Taking their cue from the caliphs, the merchants and wealthy bureaucrats competed amongst themselves to finance these projects. In this way, ancient Greek knowledge emerged from obscurity. Indeed, this was how the three Banu Musa brothers decided to use the fortune they inherited from their father to have a translation made of the Greek mechanical treatises, which they used to write the first Arabic text on mechanics, *The Book of Ingenious Devices*. Dealing primarily with automatons, it became very successful among the wealthy inhabitants of Baghdad, who ordered automatons to be built as decorations for their palaces and for the amusement of their guests.

A map of the empire

Caliph al-Mamun made frequent visits to the House of Wisdom, where he listened to the scholars' discussions. Al-Mamun was as interested as they were, for he hoped that by listening in on their conversations, he would find solutions to the military and political problems that preoccupied him.

The Earth is 27,340 miles in circumference, which is approximately the same distance calculated by the empire's astronomers as early as the 9th century!

Locating the cities

One of Caliph al-Mamun's goals was to have a reliable map of his empire, which he needed in order to familiarize himself with its territory and to govern his subjects more effectively. The best way to accomplish this goal would be to determine the exact location of the cities, and how far they were from one another. He, therefore, ordered the astronomers of Baghdad to begin work on a map.

Passionate about the project of mapping out the empire, scholars began to reflect on how they could determine the location of the cities, and how the distances between them could be calculated accurately enough to put them on a map. Delving into their task, they succeeded in determining the latitude and longitude of the most important cities by observing celestial phenomena and, most importantly, the eclipses.

A more accurate map

The astronomers began work on the map ordered by the caliph by referencing a document signed by Ptolemy, a 2nd century Greek geographer. Beginning from there, they made corrections, some of which were significant. For example, they correctly drew an ocean between Africa and India. Then, they completed their map by adding the cities to it.

The author of the first book of algebra
Al-Khwarizmi (780-850)

Al-Khwarizmi, born in Baghdad in the year 780, was five years old when the throne of the Muslim Empire went to Caliph Harun al-Rashid, whose place in history was secured for three reasons: the founding of the House of Wisdom; the dispatch of ambassadors to Charlemagne to consolidate peace between the empire and the West; and his famous nightly escapades, during which he went out carousing, dressed as a common Baghdad resident. He used these outings to eavesdrop on his subjects in order to gain insight into the criticism of his rule.

Under the rule of Harun al-Rashid, the young al-Khwarizmi began his studies at one of the private elementary schools in his neighborhood. From there, he continued on to middle school. He was passionate about mathematics and astronomy, and studied all of the treatises on the subject that came from India. He was also one of the first scientists of the empire to see the Almagest, the Arabic translation from the Greek of Ptolemy's famous treatise on astronomy.

When al-Mamun, the son of Harun al-Rashid, assumed the title of caliph, the young scholar dedicated a book to him. That book was nothing less than the very first book of algebra in human history!

By doing this, al-Khwarizmi boosted the prestige of the new caliph, who was passionate about the sciences. This was a fitting way to thank him for all of the advantages he had given the young scholar, which included a generous pension. Some time later, al-Khwarizmi struck again with another extraordinary book. This book explained a revolutionary system of arithmetic invented in India: namely, the decimal system, which school children all over the world still learn today.

Near the end of his life, al-Khwarizmi devoted himself to astrology, but his predictions were not always reliable. One day, the caliph who succeeded al-Mamun asked al-Khwarizmi and other astrologers to tell him how many years he had left to live. After many calculations, the astrologers confidently announced to the caliph that he would live another fifty years. He died only ten days later!

A symbol to represent nothing: the number zero

Before al-Khwarizmi, the Arabs used many methods to write numbers and operations involving numbers, borrowing from Babyloniania, Greece, and India.

Unearthed from an Indian book

Al-Khwarizmi discovered many new mathematical tools in the translation of an Indian book. Among these was a method for representing numbers using nine digits and a strange looking symbol that resembled a large dot: namely a zero. The Babylonians, the Greeks, and the Indians all understood the concept of zero–they knew it meant *nothing*. They did not often use it in their calculations, however, and it was al-Khwarizmi who understood and widely implemented the use of this symbol. Having decided to promote this mathematical tool, he wrote a book on arithmetic and the digits from 0 to 9, which was later translated into Latin. Zero was adopted in Europe, and then by mathematicians all over the world.

Addition and subtraction: inventing the basic operations

In his famous book on Indian arithmatic, al-Khwarizmi explained the basic operations: addition, subtraction, multiplication, and division. By

As the printing press would not be invented until the end of the 15th century in Europe, the manuscripts sold in the marketplace were hand-copied.

establishing the basics of how equations work in laypersons terms, al-Khwarizmi created a new field called algebra (from the Arabic *al-jabr*, meaning "reunion"). But that's not all! Through no effort of his own, he gave the world another mathematical term: *algorithm*, which is how Europeans mispronounced his name.

TO EACH HIS ZERO

The Babylonians represented zero with a blank space, but how do you indicate the absence or presence of a blank space without confusing yourself and your readers?

• The Greeks represented zero using the letter gamma: U.

• The Indians chose to use a period.

• The Muslims alternated between a point and a circle in their calculations.

REAL COUNTING!

0 9 8 7 6 5 4 3 2 1

٠ ٩ ٨ ٧ ٦ ٥ ٤ ٣ ٢ ١

YOUR TURN!

Careful, the numbers read from left to right:

$$
\begin{array}{r}
١٢١ \\
+ ٤٣٠ \\
\hline
\end{array}
$$

$$
\begin{array}{r}
٩٥ \\
- ١٢ \\
\hline
\end{array}
$$

$$
\begin{array}{r}
٨٧ \\
+ \quad\;\; \\
\hline
١١١
\end{array}
$$

Gerbert d'Aurillac, the astronomer and mathematician—who later became Pope Sylvester II, is thought to have been the first European to encounter Arabic numerals during a trip to Spain in the 10th century. Up until then, only Roman numerals had been used in the West.

Better know your arithmetic, or you might get ripped off

Across the vast Muslim Empire, there were many official forms of currency, such as the dinar, the silver dirham, and the copper fals, not to mention many others used by smaller kingdoms. Consequently, one's calculations had best be right!

Powerful merchants organized caravans and chartered ships all the way to China, but they did not often make the journey themselves. Instead, they sent their associates from one end of the continent to the other to sell, buy, or trade their wares. Here, as well, knowing arithmetic was essential because the middleman had to give 75% of the amount earned to the merchant, while keeping 25% for himself.

29

10th century Cairo
Alhazen: master of light

In the 7th century, Muslim horsemen from Arabia conquered Egypt. By the end of the 10th century, however, it came under the control of a different group of Muslims, this time from the Maghreb. They built their capital, Cairo, just a stone's throw from the pyramids at Giza, as a symbol of their newly acquired power.

Cairo: a rival to Baghdad

From the moment of Cairo's founding, its caliphs were in competition with those of Baghdad. Up until then, Baghdad had been the largest city in an immense empire that stretched from Spain to Central Asia. The new caliphs in Cairo wished to prove to the world, and particularly to Baghdad, that they were powerful enough to rule over all Muslims.

Within the new city, grand mosques, such as al-Azhar and al-Hakim were constructed. Their minarets still dominate the city's skyline. It was also important for Cairo to be secured militarily, so Egypt's new rulers surrounded the city with an imposing fortification, which was entered through enormous doors that would stand the test of time.

Even today, it is easy to get lost in the narrow streets of the souk that surrounds the al-Azhar Mosque. Originally, only the sale of dignified products was allowed near a mosque.

Cairo sought to attract artists and scholars in its attempt to surpass Baghdad—a goal that was accomplished in only a few decades. Scientists gathered at the House of Knowledge in Cairo, which shone as brightly as the House of Wisdom in the Baghdad of old.

The empire's second city

At the end of the 10th century, al-Hakim was named caliph at the age of eleven and ruled over a prosperous Egypt. Cairo grew in power because it was heavily populated and received steady supplies from the peasants working the fertile banks of the Nile. During the reign of al-Hakim, the city was adorned with palaces surrounded by gardens, schools, and madrasas. Cairo, thus, became the empire's second city.

The scholar who feigned madness
Alhazen (965-1040)

Ibn al-Haytham—Alhazen in Latin—was born in 965 in Basra (in present-day Iraq), which was a large, sophisticated, and tolerant city at the time. It was not uncommon to encounter a poet singing the praises of wine, for example.

At a very young age, Alhazen began to devote himself to geometry, arithmetic, optics, astronomy, and Greek philosophy from the 4th century BCE. His talent attracted the regional governor's attention, and he was invited to come and work for him. Alhazen, however, preferred to continue his work as an independent researcher. Since refusing such an offer was not easy to do without reprisal, Alhazen came up with a trick: he would feign madness while secretly preparing his escape.

Far from there, the Caliph al-Hakim of Cairo, on hearing of Alhazen's accomplishments, sent an emissary to invite him to study in Egypt. A deal was struck! The caliph himself greeted the young scholar at the gates of the city.

One day, al-Hakim summoned Alhazen and asked him to solve the problem posed by the swelling of the Nile, which regularly flooded the surrounding lands. The scholar traveled all the way to Aswan with a team of engineers to inspect the flow of the river.

The Nile traces a lifeline across the African continent all the way from Lake Victoria to the Mediterranean Sea. It irrigates Rwanda, Burundi, Tanzania, Uganda, Ethiopia, Sudan, and Egypt.

Throughout his travels, he admired the pyramids of the pharaohs, and wondered how such solid monuments could have been built. In the face of such perfection, Alhazen arrived at the following conclusion: if, with all of their ancestral know-how (sadly lost), the pharaohs' engineers were not able to dam the Nile, then the caliph's engineers would not be able to either.

Upon returning to Cairo, Alhazen had to report to the caliph. Though brave, he was not foolish, and instead of announcing that the project was impossible, he once again preferred to feign madness (this was becoming a mania!). He was placed under house arrest, where he remained until the death in 1021 of Caliph al-Hakim, who was the truly crazy one!

No sooner had the caliph been buried, then Alhazen resumed his studies. It is said that he had to support himself by copying manuscripts and selling them. His admirers also helped him through their patronage, and he continued to teach, write, and recopy his beloved Greek authors up until his death in 1040.

The mystery of the pyramids' construction was a riddle that people obsessed over for hundreds of years before it was solved in the 20th century.

How to make a rainbow:
one of Alhazen's experiments

Though fascinated by the phenomenon of light all his life, Alhazen was never able to explain the formation of rainbows.

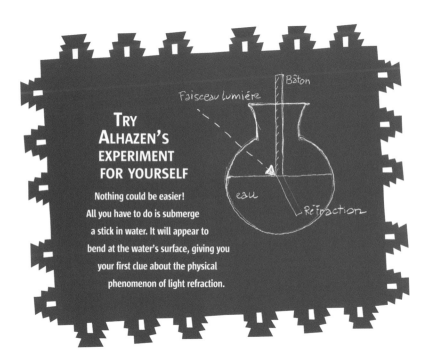

TRY ALHAZEN'S EXPERIMENT FOR YOURSELF

Nothing could be easier! All you have to do is submerge a stick in water. It will appear to bend at the water's surface, giving you your first clue about the physical phenomenon of light refraction.

A revolutionary technique

Alhazen advanced the sciences through his theories and methodology. He is considered the first researcher to treat the process of experimentation as a scientific research method. He advised his students to observe and to experiment, but also to reflect on things in an abstract way. Today, this seems self-evident, but at the time, it was revolutionary.

A successful experiment

After many failed attempts at understanding the refraction of light, Alhazen created a crystal ball that he filled with liquid. All that remained was to study, from any angle, the light rays passing through the ball.

An incomplete result

These observations led him to direct his attention to rainbows, which, in nature, are impossible to observe at will. Not only must there be simultaneous rain and sunshine, but they are only visible from a particular place at a particular time. Alhazen therefore attempted to reproduce this natural phenomenon in a laboratory setting, a task at which he didn't succeed. However, while he was unable to give a satisfactory explanation of rainbows, in the process of studying them, he created an invaluable set of tools for future researchers.

The creation of a rainbow

The creation of a rainbow was finally explained in the 13th century: in the Muslim Empire by al-Farisi, and concurrently in Europe by Dietrich de Freiburg. This is what they discovered:

Although sunlight appears to be white, it is actually a mixture of every color in the spectrum. A raindrop—or a crystal ball—will separate the colors and reflect rays of colored light in all directions.

When it rains, sunlight is refracted by millions of raindrops, each of which reflects different-colored rays of light in many directions. The eye is only able to perceive the rays of light coming directly towards it, so it sees rays of red light from the raindrops located highest up in the rainbow, yellow light from those in the middle, and blue light from the rainbow's lowest point. Together, these different colors of light form a rainbow.

To conduct his experiments, Alhazen asked glassblowers to create objects based on his sketches. In particular, he needed crystal balls and mirrors of varying shape.

Managing water in order to live

In the arid climate found in many regions of the empire, water collection was vital.

On the banks of the Nile, people lived right alongside hippopotami, which bathed in the water or buried themselves in the mud, as well as birds, which planted their feet in the water and hid themselves among the papyrus or reeds.

Finding and diverting water

Engineers sought the most effective methods for harnessing and distributing water, and the different hydraulic systems they came up with bore testament to their ingenuity. The *noria* is a good example of their technology: first, a giant wheel was powered either by an animal, or by the force of the water's current. This wheel allowed water to be drawn up from the soil or the subsoil. The water could then be delivered to fields via aqueducts and canals. Norias were common throughout the empire.

A desert miracle: the Nile

Egypt is practically a desert, but it is also fortunate enough to be traversed by the Nile, which, at approximately 4,000 miles, is one of the longest rivers in the world. It reaches its widest point near Cairo, making the entire region rich and fertile.

Modifying the shoreline under the caliph's watchful eye

Canals were built to carry water from the Nile's shoreline all the way to the fields that were to be irrigated. The caliph's bureaucrats carefully monitored canal maintenance and ensured that water was equally distributed among all landowners. At a time when famine was a constant threat, this approach to irrigation produced enough wheat to feed the inhabitants of Cairo and its surrounding countryside, and even to sell abroad. Many peasants also had vegetable gardens on the banks of the river.

Precious water
comes at a price

Although the Nile's flooding caused destruction for millennia, it was still always seen as a renewed blessing when it occurred each year.

A welcome flood

From July to October, the Nile became swollen from the annual rainfall at its source. The river water left the riverbed, overflowing and flooding its shorelines. The water was full of a black mud called silt, a veritable natural fertilizer that enriched the earth.

Rebuilding year after year, Cairo mastered geometry along the way

Agricultural lands were inundated with each flooding, and entire chunks of land were carried off by the river flow. Once the flooding had subsided, the surface area of the land had to be remeasured in order to rebuild. Without this re-measuring, it would have been impossible to determine the tax owed to the State by each landowner on the yearly harvest! This is how Cairo became foremost in surveying and geometry.

When the Nile fell too low, disaster was sure to follow

If the Nile didn't flood sufficiently for several years in a row, then the crops would die. This meant the spread of hunger in Cairo, which often fomented rebellion against the city's rulers.

The Nile's periodic flooding was carefully observed at the nilometer of Fustat, which was located near Cairo.

It was not until the 20th century that it was possible to regulate the Nile's flood plane through the construction of a dam at Aswan. Shortly thereafter, however, an unfortunate side effect was noted: native plants and animals were threatened by the drying of the riverbank.

11th century Esfahan
Avicenna completes his book of medicine

The city of Esfahan is located in central Persia (in present-day Iran). This region was part of the Muslim Empire from the beginning, and Persia was ostensibly under the rule of the Baghdad Caliphate, to whom its citizens paid taxes. The reality was far more complex, however, as many smaller kingdoms emerged throughout the region that were ruled by princes and kings who enjoyed a great deal of autonomy.

Esfahan: at the crossroads of the Muslim Empire

The high roads of the Muslim Empire crisscrossed the entire territory, leading from Spain to the steppes of Asia, and from the Sudan to the Volga (present-day Russia). All sorts of travelers populated these roads: pilgrims, both Christian and Muslim, regularly passed one another; soldiers and spies sometimes seized them; and scholars and merchants rubbed elbows. There was an unbroken stream of caravans, some of which could include up to 6,000 camels and were literally teeming with people. Along the way, man and beast alike would make several stops at a caravansary—a fortified inn built in the countryside that provided an oasis on the outskirts of the city.

Trading and business

The most famous trade routes in the world passed through Esfahan, including the Silk Road, which linked Rome to China and covered a roundtrip journey of over 8,500 miles (most merchants rarely traveled the entire route).

Esfahan echoed with conversations and business dealings in dozens of languages. While their dromedaries and camels rested up after being relieved of their heavy loads, the merchants conducted their business. They sold their cargo of precious gems and metals, amber, ivory, and lacquer, spices, glass and metal objects. Chinese silk, the most prized of all, was traded for magnificent Persian rugs.

Much like the great caliphs of the empire, the princes of Esfahan sought to populate their courts with the most brilliant scientists by providing them with a comfortable lifestyle in exchange for their knowledge. Thanks to these researchers, great progress was made, particularly in the medical field. Rivalry even developed between Esfahan and Bukhara, which had a famous hospital.

To this day, the splendor of the Blue Mosque looms in the sky above Esfahan.

The doctor adventurer
Ibn Sina, known as Avicenna (980-1037)

Avicenna was born in 980 in a small town near the big city of Bukhara—at the time in Persia (now in Uzbekistan). He was a genius from a very young age according to his autobiography, which, it must be said, is devoid of all modesty. By the age of ten, he knew the Koran by heart. It was at this point, he says, that his father "decided to send me to a greengrocer who knew arithmetic, so that I could learn from him." Next came geometry, logic, and philosophy: "I could solve any problem that my mentor proposed better than he himself was able to do." By the age of sixteen, he was already thought of as a capable doctor: "Medicine is not among the difficult sciences, and it is a field where I demonstrated my superiority enough so that competent doctors where soon under my tutelage; moreover, I was, in fact, already treating the sick."

Authorized by a local ruler to study the books in his library, Avicenna secluded himself there for two years, after which he took up residence in another court, where he had regular contact with many other scholars. Around the year 1012,

the Sultan Mahmud of Ghazni asked him to come and pay him a visit. Avicenna, however, refused the offer and was forced to flee the sultan's wrath. The sultan's police force was soon hot on his trail, and, in his fury, the sultan even disseminated a "mug shot" that was based on a painting done several years earlier. Nevertheless, the sultan's efforts were in vain.

From 1014 to 1020, Avicenna lived in various Persian cities. While he liked medicine, he also liked politics and served as vizier to a local king named Shams al-Daula. When the king's army revolted, Avicenna was imprisoned. It is possible that he began work on his most famous book, *The Canon of Medicine*, while behind bars. Once free, he settled down in Esfahan, but his hectic life, his adventures in politics, and his bon vivant lifestyle had left him with ruined health. As a doctor, Avicenna knew that his body was succumbing to disease. From 1034 onward, he gave up medicine, and, quite philosophically, he prepared to die.

Avicenna, who liked to test out his remedies, wondered if garlic could counter the effects of snake venom.

Avicenna
and the birth of science-based medicine

Avicenna traveled all over Persia at the invitation of princes and kings. To lighten his load, he learned books by heart!

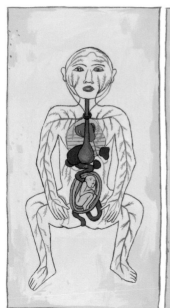

This image of a pregnant woman is included in a treatise on the development of the human fetus, which combines scholarly reason with traditional teachings from the Koran. Very early on, doctors were already generating surprisingly accurate diagrams of the human skeleton.

An indispensible book

Avicenna was simultaneously a doctor, a philosopher, a mathematician, and an astronomer. He maintained relations with scholars from several fields, and was the first Muslim doctor to treat medicine as a science. He rediscovered the theories of Hippocrates and Galen from ancient Greece, and decided to assemble all of the knowledge regarding medicine that was available at the time into his *Canon of Medicine*. Not only was this book used by all Muslims, it was also included in the curricula of European universities for the next 300 years. The treatment of the sick thus continued to follow Avicenna's recommendations for a long while.

A prodigious writer

Avicenna was always traveling and rarely had time to spend in libraries, so he took advantage of his exceptional memory to dictate his own works without recourse to any dictionary or guide. In this way, he produced fifty pages a day and authored over two hundred scientific and philosophical treatises.

In the 11th century, there were over 200 plants identified as "simple" medicines, meaning they could be swallowed or applied directly to the skin.

A mobile classroom

Avicenna's students were obligated to travel with him if they wanted access to his teachings. Avicenna knew full well that poems were easier to remember than lessons, so he employed a technique used by other teachers of the time: he wrote poetry that contained all of the information that a medical student would need. His most famous poem is over a thousand verses long, and without the help of scholars who know how to decipher it, there is no point in attempting to understand what it says!

Avicenna's discoveries

Avicenna learned how to treat lung diseases and certain types of mental illness. He was also the first to recommend the use of tools to facilitate childbirth. He preferred teaching and thinking to practicing medicine, however.

A wide array of cures

Muslim doctors divided illnesses into two categories: mental and physical. All sorts of remedies were devised that combined science and belief.

The importance of hygiene

Before choosing from among the many available treatments, doctors tried to be as specific as possible in identifying their patient's illness. When an illness was not serious, the doctor recommended exercise or a visit to the hammam. He might also have recommended a change of diet, favoring a certain type of food. Sugar, for example, was prescribed for indigestion, and because pharmacists found that it acted as a preservative, it was used as an additive in many medicines. Consequently, sugarcane was cultivated throughout the empire.

Of gazelles, mice, and ants

When a patient was very sick, the researchers first examined his urine, and then took his pulse. Each type of irregular pulse was given a name: The pulse of a gazelle indicated a burning fever; the pulse of a mouse indicated that the body was in a state of decay; and finally, the pulse of an ant occurred when a person had fainted as a result of some great anguish.

Magic and the will of God

To treat patients as best they could, doctors sometimes relied on magic. For example, they would not have hesitated to recommend the

consumption of scorpions or boiled earthworms as a remedy for bladder problems. This type of treatment was a reflection of the beliefs of the time: every rock, plant, and animal was thought to have healing powers.

The doctor himself was thought to be an instrument of God, and it was believed that God alone had the power to cure or not to cure someone who was sick.

LOVESICKNESS

This disease was easy to identify: all you had to do was to say the name of the beloved, and the patient's pulse accelerated.

THE PROPHET'S DIAGNOSIS

Muhammad's teachings included health and wellness advice, much of which remains legitimate by today's standards. To wit: "Do not overexpose yourself to the sun, because this is harmful to the skin."

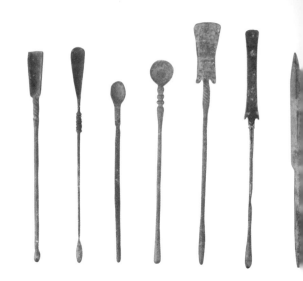

This patient cannot breathe because his throat is blocked by a tumor, so a surgeon opens a hole in his windpipe to let air in. This is an operation that is still performed today!

A true research hospital

Beginning in the 8th century, medical consultations in the Muslim Empire took place, as they do today, in private homes, doctor's offices, or at the hospital.

This patient cannot breathe because his throat is blocked by a tumor, so a surgeon opens a hole in his windpipe to let air in. This is an operation that is still performed today!

Every major Muslim city had hospitals: fifty years after its founding, Baghdad already had two. In 13th century Cairo, nurses' salaries, beds, and mattresses were all paid for directly by the sultan. The patients were separated into four different rooms, according to their type of affliction: fever, injuries, gastrointestinal problems, and vision problems, and each room was supplied with water. There was a fifth room for women, and every hospital was equipped with a pharmacy.

On the road to modern medicine

Medicine advanced quickly in the hospital setting. The head physician taught class on the premises, and the doctors discussed the most serious cases among themselves, while the students, who assisted in consultations, listened in. This approach, which is still used today, was truly novel for the time.

Treating mental illness with music

Hospitals also took in people with mental illness, which in itself was revolutionary. While

Support for hospitals

The caliphs and other rulers sought to surround themselves with good doctors, and the way to attract doctors was to finance the construction of hospitals. By doing so, the caliphs also hoped to appease their populations and avoid rebellion. Moreover, charitable acts were recommended by the Prophet as a way to guarantee the salvation of the soul after death.

44

The tools of a surgeon include scissors, scalpels, and lancets; battle wounds, sores, and dental abscesses were cauterized with red-hot irons.

In the Muslim Empire, the word for hospital is *bimaristan*, which means, "house of the sick."

In Avicenna's time, pharmacists were already using a penicillin-based ointment to treat infection. The exact mechanism by which this substance worked was not known until the 20th century, when penicillin revolutionized modern medicine.

they prescribed medicines, they also believed that music could be of great benefit. On the terrace at the asylum in Aleppo (in present-day Syria) an orchestra platform was built, and seats were carved out of stone for the patients. According to both the scholars and the Prophet, however, no music could soothe the mind as effectively as "natural music," such as the sound of wind blowing through leaves, the songs of birds, and the rushing of water. This is why there was a fountain at the center of every hospital.

Opening up the body: taboo...

Very few doctors dared to open up the body to perform surgery. It was not known how to prevent infection, and anesthesia remained mild: the patient simply inhaled from a sponge saturated with opium.

...and risky

Doctors at hospitals would not perform operations; this was something they left to the surgeons, who traveled from city to city. The risk of surgery-related death was so high that surgeons may have moved around as much as they did to escape grieving family members. It is said that the famous doctor Rhazes preferred to go blind at the end of his life rather than have his eyes operated on.

The Crusades brought the idea of a hospital to Europe. At the time in the West, it was still standard practice to lock up lepers and the mentally ill as far away as possible.

12th century Palermo
Al-Idrisi maps the known world

In the 12th century, the Mediterranean, where Muslim influence had been very strong for four hundred years, came under European control.

The Mediterranean: a sea between two worlds

The Mediterranean Sea, which separated the West and East, was a passageway of great strategic importance. As such, beginning in 1095, the Christian armies that embarked on the Crusades to recapture Jerusalem from the Muslims and to conquer new territories, had to brave its crossing.

Sicily: european once again

Four years before the Crusades, the Mediterranean island of Sicily (in present-day Italy) regained its status as a Christian kingdom, after having been part of the Muslim Empire since the 10th century. Amicable relations were maintained between Christians and Muslims, however, so most Muslims remained, encouraged by the wise policy decisions of Sicily's new king, Roger II.

Palermo's port was highly sought-after by ship captains. Sea travel on the Mediterranean Sea was dangerous, both because of fearsome pirates and tempests.

He was an admirer of the original caliphs of Baghdad and wanted Palermo to become the scientific capital of the Western world.

Palermo attracts the scholars of europe

Palermo was the island's capital, and one of the most populous Mediterranean cities. At a time when education was rare in the Western world, scores of young Europeans were drawn to the scientific knowledge of the Arab scholars who gathered there. Once in Palermo, they made copies of the Greek manuscripts that they found there, and they learned Arabic so they could translate the works of the Muslim Empire.

Traveler and geographer
Al-Idrisi (born circa 1100)

Muhammad al-Idrisi was born around 1100, and grew up in Ceuta (today a Spanish enclave in Morocco). The young al-Idrisi quickly developed a desire to explore his homeland, so he crossed the sea into Muslim Spain. There he completed his studies in literature, grammar, medicine, botany, and geography. He then continued on to discover the rest of the empire. He traveled from Egypt to Asia Minor, gathering information about the countries he visited along the way. Clearly, he was well on his way to becoming a geographer!

Al-Idrisi noted that Arab geography had not yet succeeded in depicting the entire known world, so he came up with a very ambitious plan: he would create a true world map. As luck would have it, Roger II, the Christian king of Sicily, also wanted such a map, so he invited al-Idrisi to take up residence in his court. Thus, at the age of thirty-nine, the geographer put to sea once again.

The Muslim scholars and artisans who chose to remain on the island after its recapture continued their activities as before, maintaining correspondence with their colleagues elsewhere in the empire. Al-Idrisi had no difficulty in recruiting highly skilled draftsmen, painters, and mathematicians who were fluent in written and spoken Arabic to help him create his map.

Since Sicily was just off the European coastline, al-Idrisi could easily send his researchers into the Christian countries. Their mission was to verify the accuracy of what had been written by Muslim geographers up to that point regarding Europe. They were also instructed to report on new discoveries. Since his work was understandably very time consuming, it wasn't until fifteen years later that al-Idrisi handed King Roger II his world map, accompanied by a guidebook.

Al-Idrisi stayed in Palermo after the death of Roger II, but he was faced with a new problem: how to make a living as a scholar. He knew that the easiest thing would be to consecrate his work to a powerful ruler, who might then reward him with money and favors. He thus decided to dedicate his new book, *Pleasure of Men and Delight of Souls,* to the new king. Also passionate about botany, he wrote a guidebook detailing a wide variety of medicinal plants, with each plant listed by name in six languages. This enormous undertaking proved particularly valuable for pharmacists and doctors, who treated patients with the help of plants. Al-Idrisi had no margin of error in his translation, for confusing the name of a curative plant with that of a poisonous one would be disastrous! Fortunately he got it right!

Travelers and merchants resting at a caravansary.
The animals slept alongside their cargo, while
the men relaxed on the second floor.

The world
precision in mapping

Al-Idrisi's research allowed him to represent the entire world in seventy parts, including every continent except the Americas, which were unknown at the time.

The entire known world

Referencing five thousand place names, al-Idrisi described in his work, the *Book of Roger*, everything that a map cannot show. Because of his personal familiarity with the Muslim Empire, that portion of his map was extremely detailed. The kingdoms of France, England, Germany, and Italy were also included, along with the Scandinavian countries and Russia. As for the Asian countries, their geography was presented primarily in relation to the customs and activities of their inhabitants. It is thought that this information was most likely obtained through conversations with merchants and the study of letters and travel accounts.

A penchant for accuracy

For each region he included, al-Idrisi recorded the cities and villages; the distances between them; the economic activities by which they were characterized; the climate; the customs; and sometimes even the cuisine! At the time, such accuracy was a rare feat.

Under the reign of Roger II, Christians and Muslims peacefully coexisted on the island of Sicily, which was ideally located at the crossroads of maritime routes between the East and the West. This building in Palermo was a mosque before its conversion to a church.

A mix of science and legend

In the Middle Ages, all geographical works were informed by the reports of travelers and merchants, and they did not hesitate to include report of the strange and bizarre phenomena that had been observed. Even the eminently scientific al-Idrisi wrote of mysterious wonders.

For example, his book describes an island that is inhabited by "strange creatures that resemble women," to whom he refers as "Ogresses." He goes on to describe them: "their teeth protrude from their mouths, they shoot lighting bolts from their eyes, and their legs resemble burnt wood. These creatures speak an unintelligible language, and are at war with the monsters of the sea."

Amazingly, the *Book of King Roger* was unknown in the West until an Arabic version was printed in Rome in the 16th century, which was followed by the appearance of its Latin translation, published in the 17th century.

South

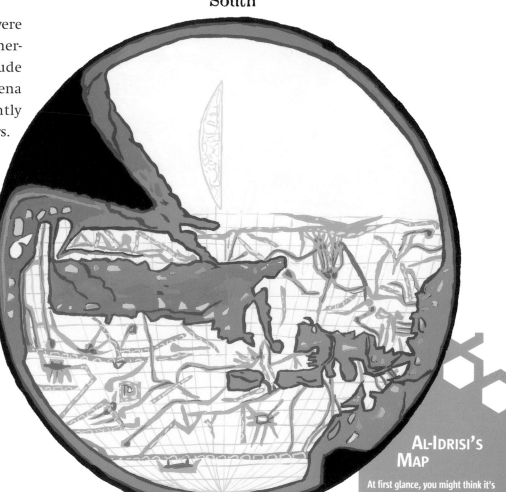

North

AL-IDRISI'S MAP

At first glance, you might think it's upside down. This is because in the Middle Ages, Muslim geographers saw the south as "up" and the north as "down." Al-Idrisi's representation of France is rather disproportionate, although you can clearly see the Breton Peninsula, which juts out into the Atlantic like a nose. You can also make out Italy, Sicily, and Greece on the opposite side of the Mediterranean Sea.

Charting a course
through the vastness of the world

Using the manuscripts of ancient Greece as their starting point, the Muslim astronomers and geographers developed their own skills and tools. Driven forward by scientific curiosity, they answered the requests of religious leaders and helped them to address their needs.

Mecca, located in Arabia, is one of the three holy cities of Islam. Every Muslim must go there, if possible, at least once. Pilgrimage begins at the Kaaba sanctuary, pictured here.

Locating Mecca

During prayer, every Muslim must face the Kaaba, which is located in Mecca. This is in accordance with the divine word of the Prophet as dictated by the Koran: "Turn your face toward the sacred mosque."

One of the very first tasks that the caliph of Baghdad assigned to his astronomers and geographers was to help believers determine the direction in which to pray, regardless of their location in the empire.

Toward this end, scholars came up with a type of compass, called the "qibla finder." The names of cities were marked in relation to their respective latitudes and longitudes. To find the right direction for prayer, you oriented a pointer to correspond to your present location, and the qibla finder would show how to orient yourself for prayer.

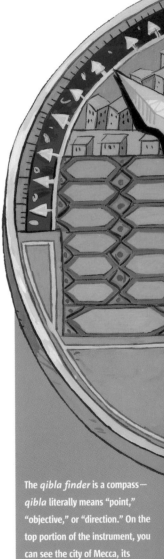

The *qibla finder* is a compass—*qibla* literally means "point," "objective," or "direction." On the top portion of the instrument, you can see the city of Mecca, its mosque, and the Kaaba sanctuary.

Longitude

Latitude

Equator

Different Arab maps

The Arab geographers developed many different types of maps: world maps that were centered on the Muslim Empire, road maps that proved invaluable for military operations or caravans, and portolans, which were used by ship captains to locate ports.

The astrolabe

The astrolabe, invented in ancient Greece, was used to calculate the time of day by measuring the positions of stars in the sky. This allowed one to orient oneself, and to produce measurements of height and depth. The Muslims perfected this complex instrument and invented other instruments, such as the universal astrolabe and the astronomical sundial, which were based on the same principles, but which were lighter and more effective.

Traditionally, the longitude of a point on Earth's surface is represented by its position in relation to a prime meridian—an imaginary line that links the North and South poles. A point's latitude is traditionally thought of as its position in relation to the equator, which is the imaginary circle around the globe's widest point.

These measurements are calculated in degrees and make it possible to locate the exact location of any point on the surface of a globe; this was a helpful reference for travelers.

The compass

The compass was first invented in China, and later adopted by Muslim sailors, who used it to navigate while at sea.

53

14th century Damascus
Ibn al-Shatir measures time

The cities of the Muslim Empire were weakened by the Crusades, a series of battles and sieges launched by the Christian kingdoms of the West. Although these were over by the end of the 13th century, it was then that a new danger appeared: the constant threat from the Mongols of Asia, who were led by the famous warlord, Genghis Khan.

The Mongols invade the cities

Baghdad, which had been the empire's dazzling capital at the beginning of the Muslim era, fell to the Mongols at the end of the 13th century. The caliph was executed, and the wealthiest citizens were massacred, thus ending the age of the Muslim Empire. The Mongols moved on to invade and pillage Damascus (in present-day Syria). Its decimated neighborhoods were rebuilt little by little, and daily life eventually resumed. By the 14th century, Damascus had become a bustling and vibrant city once again.

Ahead of its time

Working with iron and glass, producing instruments, cosmetics, and humble bars of soap, the artisans of Damascus used techniques that were highly sophisticated for the time. The sciences were also very active, with the city boasting ninety madrasas, where students attended seminars conducted by top professors from all over the region. Hospitals were also places of learning; when doctors weren't caring for patients, they, too, were sharing their knowledge.

Less wealthy, but still great

In the 14th century, the risk of a new Mongol invasion was of constant concern to Damascus and its rival cities. As with all of its neighbors, Damascus was less wealthy than before. Although European forces had been definitively rebuffed from the Middle East, they, nevertheless, had gained dominance of the international trade routes of the Mediterranean, formerly under Muslim control. Still, Damascus was fortunate enough to be the capital of an enormous province that would later become Syria.

Astronomers would often climb to the highest point in the city to get the best possible view of the sky. This may have been a hilltop, or, in the case of Damascus, a minaret.

55

Stargazing
Ibn al-Shatir (born circa 1304)

Ibn al-Shatir was born in Damascus around 1304, under a bad sign: his father died when he was only six years old. Luckily, one of his uncles, a renowned artisan, took him in and taught him his craft. Ibn al-Shatir thus became a master at crafting ivory, wood, and enamel. In addition to his scientific work, he continued to create works of art throughout his life.

As an adolescent, his uncle also taught him geometry, arithmetic, and astronomy. Upon becoming an adult, al-Shatir moved to Cairo, where he immersed himself in the astronomical treatises of his predecessors. He was particularly taken with the work of a certain rainbow enthusiast: Alhazen.

Ibn al-Shatir became a leading astronomer. Although he could often be found with his nose in a book, or gazing at the stars, he was also a prolific inventor. Some of his works were theoretical, while others were essentially instructional guides or manuals, in which he explained the instruments of astronomical observation that he had created. These practical guides allowed his colleagues to create their own tools, using his inventions as a template. What a generous man al-Shatir was!

It is said that the Umayyad Mosque was built at the beginning of the 7th century in the most sacred part of Damascus because it stands on the very foundation of what had been the church of Saint John the Baptist, dating back to the 4th century. This church was itself built on top of an ancient Roman temple devoted to Jupiter.

On his return to Damascus, the astronomer was appointed to the position of muwaqqit, meaning "timekeeper," at the Grand Umayyad Mosque. His job was to calculate the exact time of each of the five daily Muslim prayers. He quickly ascended the ranks of the muwaqqits, with his practical nature leading him to the creation of a sundial labeled with each of the five prayer times. This was placed well within view of one of the mosque's minarets.

Ibn al-Shatir was now finally free to relax, but he did nothing of the kind. Instead, he invented an astronomical clock that he hung on the wall of his home so that he could tell the position of the sun and stars whenever he wanted.

At the time of his death in 1375, knowledge of Ibn al-Shatir's inventions had spread all the way to Europe. For example, Copernicus, the great 15th-century Polish astronomer, knew of them. Today, having survived the passage of time, some of his inventions can be viewed at either the Paris Observatory or the French National Library.

To understand the universe, to assign dates to festivals and fasts, to determine the direction of Mecca, or to predict the future, astronomers interpreted the sky.

The queen of the sciences

How does the universe work? This is the question that medieval astronomy in Europe, the Muslim World, and elsewhere attempted to answer.

Using science to observe the sky... but why?

Astronomy was divided into two main branches: theoretical astronomy, which involved the study of the universe, and navigational astronomy, which was used for charting courses and for creating clocks and other everyday tools.

Most scientists incorporated the study of astronomy into their education. For example, the mathematician al-Khwarizmi, the physicist Alhazen, and the doctor Avicenna were all astronomers. Astronomy was the most widely practiced science in the empire.

Deciphering the world

Astronomers spent most of their time observing the sky, with the objective of understanding how the universe works. Establishing the position of the Earth among the other planets and stars was a major undertaking and represented a deeper question: What is humankind's place in the universe?

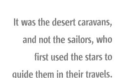

It was the desert caravans, and not the sailors, who first used the stars to guide them in their travels.

Humans have always strived for understanding—both of the present and the future. Through the 17th century, in both the Muslim and the Christian worlds, there was no distinction drawn between astrology and astronomy. Astrology was considered an extension of astronomy because stars were thought to predict fate. Muslims were even influenced by the practice of Indian astrology, some of whose symbols are pictured here:

THE UNIVERSE ACCORDING TO PTOLEMY

In 2nd century Greece, Ptolemy proposed the hypothesis that the Earth rests motionless at the center of the universe. This idea was widely debated and remained a point of astronomical controversy until the 15th century.

Jupiter

Venus

Mars

Mercury

Earth

Moon

Sun

Saturn

THE UNIVERSE ACCORDING TO COPERNICUS

In Europe, the Polish astronomer, Copernicus, who knew certain treatises of Muslim astronomy very well, was the first scientist to realize that the Earth rotates around the sun as well as around its own axis at the same time.

Jupiter

Moon

Mars

Earth

Saturn

Sun

Mercury

Venus

Observing the vastness of the universe

During the time of Ibn al-Shatir, astronomers did their work without the aid of astronomical glasses, which were invented several centuries later in Europe in the form of powerful binoculars or telescopes that made it possible to see the sky "up close." All of their observation was done with the naked eye, aided only by a simple cone that shielded their vision from the sun. They did, however, use a variety of instruments, such as astrolabes or astronomical sundials, which were used to measure how high the stars were in the sky.

Muslim scientists were ahead of their Western colleagues for a long time. Consequently, many of the names that they gave to stars and constellations are those that are still used all over the world to this day. Vega, Aldebaran, Altair, and Betelgeuse are some examples.

Stars, letters, and math

To guide their research, the astronomers used the writings of the Greek scholar, Ptolemy, in addition to those of their Muslim compatriots. Because their field required advanced arithmetic, they benefitted by reading mathematical treatises, and they adhered to notions of geometry, such as cosine and tangent, as they calculated the positions of celestial bodies, and the "baseline" coordinates: the latitude and longitude of the Earth's surface. In this way, astronomy played an important role in the development of geography.

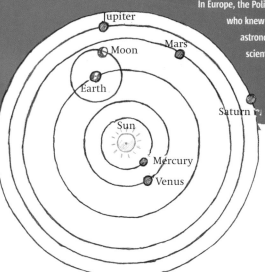

The Arabians were given to observing the sky even before the founding of Islam. The scientific golden age produced observatories throughout the empire.

Putting their knowledge to work

Thanks to the discipline of astronomy, people were able to incorporate concepts of space and time into their daily activities.

An applied science

As a result of the work done by both astronomers and other scholars, it was possible for a caliph to examine the entire expanse of his empire by simply glancing at a map of the known world. Likewise, a landowner could survey his fields, and people were able to synchronize their daily activities by measuring time in terms of years, months, days, and hours.

These new possibilities were arrived at through the use of measurement tools that astronomers invented by drawing upon all of their knowledge regarding the movement of the stars in the sky over either a twenty-four hour period or the changing seasons. Mathematics and complex technical operations allowed this knowledge to be applied in the creation of calendars and clocks.

How long will winter last?

Muslim scholars were zealous about tracking the sun's annual trajectory, and they sought to discover whether Ptolemy's calculations, worked out in ancient times, would still hold true. They therefore recalculated the slant of the sun's trajectory in order to discover the exact length of the seasons.

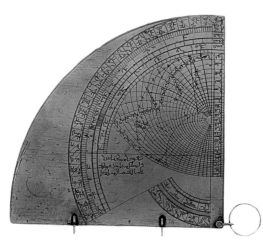

The easiest way to measure a star's position in the sky was to use an astrological sundial.

WHAT TIME IS IT?

While it was possible to calculate the time using an houglass in the 14th century, it was also cumbersome and inaccurate. Another option was to use a water clock, which was expensive. The better option was to use a gnomon, which is simply a stick protruding from a wall, where the position of the shadow cast by the stick indicates the time of day. Sundials function in much the same way as gnomons, but because they are built according to rigorous calculations, they are more accurate.

"A little knowledge is worth more than a lot of superstition."

Such was the word of the Prophet himself. In keeping with this, the successive caliphs (the great religious leaders of all of the Muslims) often solicited the help of astronomers.

The astronomers did far more than simply determine the direction of Mecca or calculate the exact times of the five daily prayers. They also studied the cycles of the moon, which vary from year to year, and marked them on calendars. This allowed them to create a new calendar at the beginning of each year, making it possible to determine the exact date on which the month of Ramadan— the annual month-long Muslim fast—would begin.

IBN AL-SHATIR'S SUNDIAL: A CONSTANT THROUGH CENTURIES OF CHANGE

Ibn al-Shatir's sundial, located within the courtyard of the Umayyad Mosque in Damascus, tracked the unwavering course of the sun for so long that it stirs the imagination to think about it. Quite another feeling arises at the thought that while the sun shone down on the land, the violence of humanity continued in its course. Although Damascus recovered from the first Mongol attack in the 13th century, the second attack, in the 15th century, marked the beginning of its decline. The most talented artists and craftsmen were sent to Samarkand, the Mongol capital, to enrich the enormous construction projects underway there. The sundial that can be seen today in Damascus is a copy of the original, which was destroyed in the 19th century.

The Greeks were the first to propose using a globe to represent the earth from above. The Muslims consulted manuscripts from India before they began to create their own globes, which improved upon earlier versions.

GLOSSARY

Al - In the Arabic language, "al" means "the." It is a word frequently encountered in proper nouns. For example, the mathematician al-Khwarizmi's name literally means, "The Khwarizmi" —Khwarezm being a region in Central Asia. **pp. 23, 26, 47, 48.**

Ancient Greece - During antiquity, (the period between prehistory and the Middle Ages), the inhabitants of Greece built a glorious culture.So glorious, in fact, that it radiated out all over the Mediterranean, influencing the civilizations that succeeded it for hundreds of years to come. Many traces of this culture remain even today: our way of living together (the Greeks invented the word citizen); the Olympic Games; and their mythology, including such gods as Zeus and Aphrodite, who live on in literature and works of art. **pp. 18, 24, 53.**

Andalusia - Today, Andalusia is one of the regions of Spain. The word Andalusia is derived from the name *al-Andalus,* which, from the 8th - 15th century, referred to the portion of present-day Spain belonging to the Muslim Empire. **pp. 10, 13.**

Aristotle - (384-322 BCE.) The greatest of all ancient Greek philosophers, he dedicated his life to observing nature,

people, and the cities they built. **pp. 18, 32.**

Astrolabe - This instrument is used to measure time, to orient oneself, and to carry out measurements in surveying (height of buildings, depth of pits, width of rivers, etc.). **pp. 53, 59**.

Astrology - The art of predicting the future based on the position and placement of the stars in the sky. **pp. 22, 26, 58.**

Astronomy - The study of the shape, position, and movement of the celestial bodies, such as planets and stars. **pp. 5, 25, 26, 56, 58, 59.**

Byzantium - In the Middle Ages, the city of Istanbul (present-day Turkey) was called Byzantium, and it was the capital of an enormous Christian empire that was the successor to the Roman Empire from the 5th to the 15th century. **pp. 4, 10, 11, 18, 24.**

Caliphate - This word signifies both a territory under the rule of a caliph, and the political regime itself. This is why we refer both to the caliphate of Harun al-Rashid, and to the Abbasid caliphate of Baghdad. **pp. 13.**

Caliph - The word caliph means "successor to Muhammad" and is used

to denote the political leader of all Muslims and of the Muslim Empire from the 8th to the 15th century. **pp. 10, 13, 15, 16, 17, 23, 29, 32, 39, 44, 61.**

Caravan - A group of merchants who pooled together their beasts of burden—dromedaries, mules, and horses—in order to travel or transport their goods between oases and cities. **pp. 7, 15, 29, 39, 50, 53.**

Caravansary - A caravansary was a particular type of hotel intended for merchants traveling in caravans as well as travelers in general. Caravansaries also served as storage space for merchandise. **pp. 43, 49.**

Compass - This instrument indicates which direction is north through a magnetized needle and is used to find one's bearings. It eventually replaced the astrolabe. **pp. 53.**

Copernicus - (1473-1543) The Polish astronomer who introduced the then-revolutionary hypothesis that the Earth is not at the center of the universe, but that it rotates around the sun just like the other planets do. **pp. 56, 59.**

Crusades - The eight major campaigns led by Christians from the West into the Middle East from the 11th to the 13th century. Their goal was to recapture the city of Jerusalem (see glossary entry) from the Muslims and to conquer new lands. By the end of the 13th century, the Muslims had taken back the territory conquered through the Crusades. **pp. 5, 12, 19, 47, 55.**

Decimal System - This is the Indian numerical system that was popularized by al-Khwarizmi. Made up of nine numbers accompanied by the number zero, it is used all over the world to this day. **pp. 26.**

Dynasty - When many rulers of a certain country, for example, belong to the same family, this family is called a dynasty. The word can also refer to the period during which the family rules. **pp. 13.**

Emir - The person chosen by the caliph to serve as his representative within a portion of his territory. The word emir literally means, "keeper of order." **pp. 14, 15.**

Euphrates - The source of this Asian river is located in a Turkish mountain range. It is 1,787 miles long, and provides irrigation to the Fertile Crescent. **pp. 23**.

Fertile Crescent - This refers to the vast region that is irrigated by the Tigris and the Euphrates (see glossary entries) where humans first settled and gave up the nomadic way of life. This is where writing was later invented, and, even later still, the three major monotheistic religions: Judaism, Christianity, and Islam. The word crescent refers to the region's shape.

Galen - (131-201) was the great ancient Greek doctor and one of the founders of the medical field. He devoted much of his life to the development of an encyclopedia containing the knowledge of his time. He was also a great teacher, and his methods influenced medieval Muslim, Jewish, and Christian medicine. **pp. 42.**

Genghis Khan - (circa 1162-1227) He founded the first Mongol Empire in 12th century Central Asia. A great warrior, he took control of northern China in 1211, and went on to invade Russia and Afghanistan. **pp. 55.**

Geography - In Greek, geography means "to describe the Earth." Geography is the science that studies the elements of Earth's surface along with the places inhabited by human beings. **pp. 25, 48, 50, 51, 59.**

Hippocrates - (460-circa 370 BCE) This great doctor of ancient Greece recommended the systematic observation of a patient's symptoms before giving a diagnosis. To this day doctors follow his advice, reciting what is called, "the Hippocratic Oath," an official declaration of their dedication to serving their patients and maintaining their health. **pp. 42.**

Ibn - In Arabic, this means "son of," and often appears in people's names. For example, the great astronomer, Ibn al-Shatter's name means "son of a dexterous man." **pp. 40, 55, 56.**

Islam - Islam is the name of the Muslim religion. It is a monotheistic (see glossary entry) religion, revealed to the Prophet Muhammad in the 7th century. **pp. 4, 6, 7, 8, 9, 17.**

Jerusalem - Jerusalem is the "thrice holy" city because it is the location of the holiest site in Judaism—the Wailing Wall; the holiest Christian site—the Church of the Holy Sepulcher; and the third most important holy site in Islam—the Dome of the Rock. **pp. 5, 10, 47.**

Kaaba - The Kaaba is the cube-shaped monument located at the center of Mecca. At the beginning of the pilgrimage, everyone must circle it seven times. **pp. 7, 52.**

Koran - This is the name of the Muslim holy book. It relates the word of God as revealed through the Prophet Muhammad. **pp. 8, 9, 10, 16, 40, 42, 53.**

Latitude - Along with longitude, it is one of the two baselines used to determine the position of a point in the sky or on the Earth's surface. It is measured in degrees beginning at the equator. **pp. 25, 52, 53, 59.**

Longitude - Along with latitude, it is one of the two baselines used to determine the position of a point in the sky or on the Earth's surface. It is measured in degrees beginning at the prime meridian (see glossary entry), which is located in Greenwich, UK. **pp. 25, 52, 53, 59.**

Madrasa - A type of university, where students begin their studies at the age of sixteen, after completing elementary school. In the Muslim Empire, there was no such thing as high school; students went directly from elementary school to a madrasa. **pp.17, 31, 55.**

Maghreb - The region in Africa located north of the Sahara, stretching from present-day Libya to the Atlantic coast. The word Maghreb means "West" in Arabic. **pp. 11, 31.**

Manuscript - A hand-written text. Before the invention of the printing press by Gutenberg in the 15th century, all books were hand-written. **pp. 18, 19, 24, 32, 47.**

Mecca - In present-day Saudi Arabia, Mecca is the birthplace of Muhammad and Islam's holiest site. Every Muslim is advised to make a pilgrimage to Mecca at least once during his or her lifetime provided that he or she has the means to do so. **pp. 7, 9, 13, 17, 52, 57, 61.**

Meridian - A meridian is an imaginary line that connects all points of the same longitude situated between Earth's poles. **p. 53.**

Minaret - A minaret is the tower of a mosque. The five daily calls to prayer are made from the top of a mosque's minaret. **pp. 55, 56.**

Mongols - The Mongols were a nomadic tribe from Central Asia. They were united at the beginning of the 13th century by Genghis Khan, and founded an empire that encompassed a large part of Asia, the Fertile Crescent (see glossary entry), and part of Europe. **pp. 5, 12, 13, 55, 61.**

Monotheism - A religious doctrine that professes the existence of one and only one God. Islam, Judaism, and Christianity are all monotheistic religions.

Mosque - The building where Muslims practice their religion. **pp. 9, 16, 17, 31, 39, 50, 56.**

Muslim - The word literally means, "one who submits to God." Everyone who adheres to Islam is a Muslim. **pp. 5, 7, 8, 9, 10, 11, 13, 18, 19.**

Nile - The Nile is the longest river in Africa at 4,163 miles. Lake Victoria is its source, from which it travels through Rwanda, Burundi, Tanzania, Uganda, Ethiopia, Sudan, and Egypt. **pp. 8, 31, 32, 36, 37.**

Ptolemy - (circa 110-170) Ptolemy was a great astronomer, mathematician, and geographer who lived in ancient Greece (see glossary entry). One of his famous books, *The Almagest*, written in 140, was translated into Arabic in the 8th century, and then into Latin in the 12th century. This work, which hypothesized that the Earth stood immobile at the center of the universe, was accepted as canon until the 15th century. **pp. 18, 25, 26, 59, 60.**

Qibla - The qibla is the direction of Mecca toward which Muslims turn to pray. **pp. 52, 53.**

Refraction of Light - This phenomenon occurs when a ray of light passes from one medium (air, for example) to another (water, for example), and can be explained by the difference in the speed of light within each of the media through which it passes. **pp. 34.**

Sultan - The title used by the Arabs beginning in the 11th century to designate the person who holds political power. **pp. 44.**

Surveying - In geometry, to survey land means to measure it. pp. 37

Tigris - The Tigris, whose source is in Turkey, is one of the two major rivers of the Fertile Crescent (see glossary entry) region. **pp. 23.**

Vizier - This is the title given to the most important person after the caliph. **pp. 14**

BIBLIOGRAPHY

Peter Adamson & Richard C. Taylor, Editors, *The Cambridge Companion to Arabic Philosophy* (Cambridge Companions to Philosophy), Cambridge University Press, 2005

George Beshore, *Science in Early Islamic Culture* (Science of the Past) Franklin Watts, 1998.

Corona Brezina, *Al-Khwarizmi: The Inventor of Algebra* (Great Muslim Philosophers and Scientists of the Middle Ages), Rosen Central, 2006.

Dimitri Gutas, *Greek Thought, Arab Culture: The Graeco-Arabic Translation Movement in Baghdad and Early Abbasid Society (2nd-4th/8th-10th centuries)* (Arabic Thought & Culture), Routledge, 1998.

Tony Huff, The Rise of Early *Modern Science: Islam, China and the West*, Cambridge University Press, 2003.

Hugh Kennedy, *When Baghdad Ruled The Muslim World: The Rise and Fall of Islam's Greatest Dynasty*, Da Capo, 2005.

Hugh Kennedy, *The Great Arab Conquests: How the Spread of Islam Changed the World We Live In*, Da Capo Press, 2007.

Asha Khan, *Avicenna (Ibn Sina): Muslim Physician and Philosopher of the 11th Century* (Great Muslim Philosophers and Scientists of the Middle Ages), Rosen Central, 2006.

David Levering Lewis, *God's Crucible: Islam and the Making of Europe, 570-1215*, W.W. Norton, 2008.

Amin Maalouf, *The Crusades Through Arab Eyes*, Schocken, 1989.

James E. McClellan, *Science and Technology in World History: An Introduction*, The Johns Hopkins University Press, 2006.

Michael H. Morgan, *Lost History: The Enduring Legacy of Muslim Scientists, Thinkers, and Artists*, National Geographic, 2007

Peter E. Pormann & Emilie Savage-Smith, *Medieval Islamic Medicine*, Georgetown University Press, 2007.

George Saliba, *Islamic Science and the Making of the European Renaissance* (Transformations: Studies in the History of Science and Technology), MIT Press, 2007

George Saliba, *A History of Arabic Astronomy: Planetary Theories During the Golden Age of Islam* (New York University Studies in Near Eastern Civilization), NYU Press, 1995

Nancy G. Siraisi, *Medieval and Early Renaissance Medicine: An Introduction to Knowledge and Practice*, University of Chicago Press, 2007.

Howard R. Turner, *Science in Medieval Islam: An Illustrated Introduction*, University of Texas Press, 1997.

Photographic credits

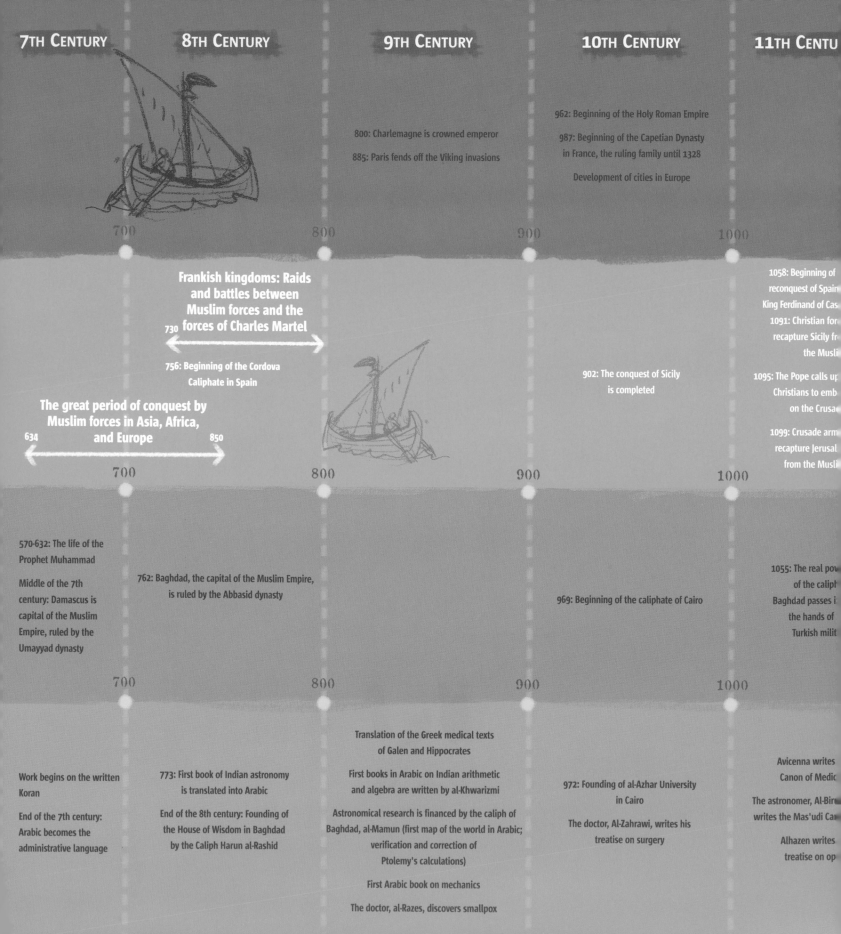

| 7TH CENTURY | 8TH CENTURY | 9TH CENTURY | 10TH CENTURY | 11TH CENTU |

800: Charlemagne is crowned emperor

885: Paris fends off the Viking invasions

962: Beginning of the Holy Roman Empire

987: Beginning of the Capetian Dynasty in France, the ruling family until 1328

Development of cities in Europe

700   800   900   1000

Frankish kingdoms: Raids and battles between Muslim forces and the forces of Charles Martel
730 ←→

756: Beginning of the Cordova Caliphate in Spain

The great period of conquest by Muslim forces in Asia, Africa, and Europe
634 ←→ 850

902: The conquest of Sicily is completed

1058: Beginning of reconquest of Spain King Ferdinand of Cas

1091: Christian for recapture Sicily fr the Musli

1095: The Pope calls up Christians to emb on the Crusa

1099: Crusade arm recapture Jerusal from the Musli

700   800   900   1000

570-632: The life of the Prophet Muhammad

Middle of the 7th century: Damascus is capital of the Muslim Empire, ruled by the Umayyad dynasty

762: Baghdad, the capital of the Muslim Empire, is ruled by the Abbasid dynasty

969: Beginning of the caliphate of Cairo

1055: The real pow of the caliph Baghdad passes i the hands of Turkish milit

700   800   900   1000

Work begins on the written Koran

End of the 7th century: Arabic becomes the administrative language

773: First book of Indian astronomy is translated into Arabic

End of the 8th century: Founding of the House of Wisdom in Baghdad by the Caliph Harun al-Rashid

Translation of the Greek medical texts of Galen and Hippocrates

First books in Arabic on Indian arithmetic and algebra are written by al-Khwarizmi

Astronomical research is financed by the caliph of Baghdad, al-Mamun (first map of the world in Arabic; verification and correction of Ptolemy's calculations)

First Arabic book on mechanics

The doctor, al-Razes, discovers smallpox

972: Founding of al-Azhar University in Cairo

The doctor, Al-Zahrawi, writes his treatise on surgery

Avicenna writes Canon of Medic

The astronomer, Al-Biru writes the Mas'udi Ca

Alhazen writes treatise on op

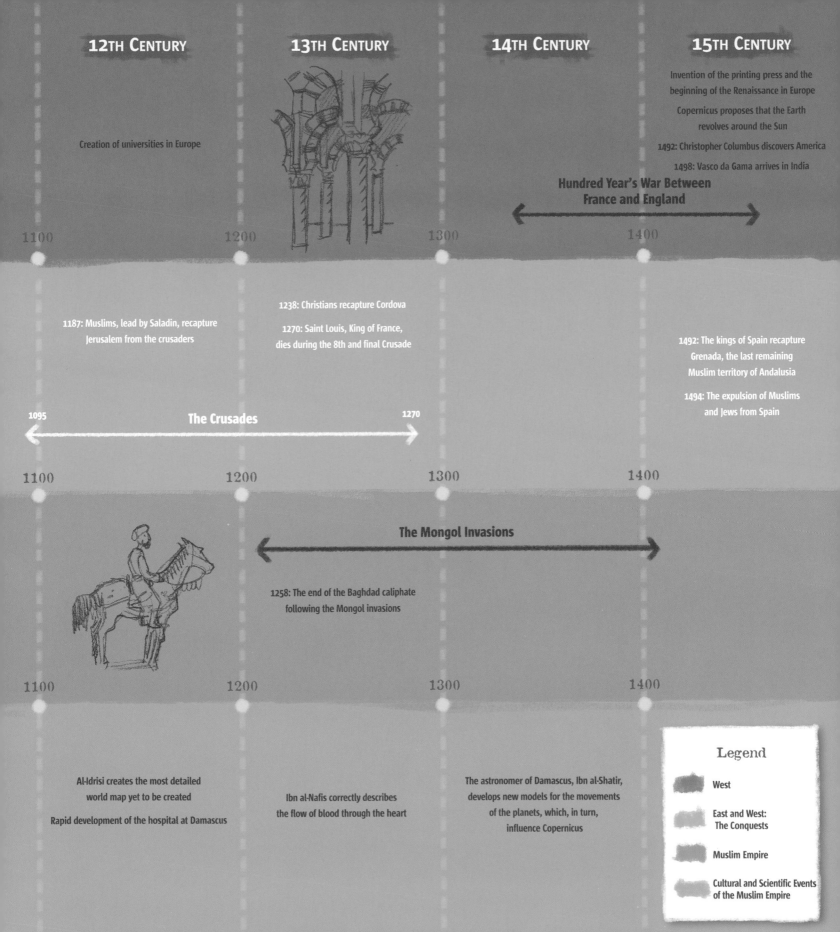

12TH CENTURY

Creation of universities in Europe

13TH CENTURY

14TH CENTURY

15TH CENTURY

Invention of the printing press and the beginning of the Renaissance in Europe

Copernicus proposes that the Earth revolves around the Sun

1492: Christopher Columbus discovers America

1498: Vasco da Gama arrives in India

Hundred Year's War Between France and England

1100 — 1200 — 1300 — 1400

1238: Christians recapture Cordova

1270: Saint Louis, King of France, dies during the 8th and final Crusade

1187: Muslims, lead by Saladin, recapture Jerusalem from the crusaders

1492: The kings of Spain recapture Grenada, the last remaining Muslim territory of Andalusia

1494: The expulsion of Muslims and Jews from Spain

1095 ← **The Crusades** → 1270

1100 — 1200 — 1300 — 1400

← **The Mongol Invasions** →

1258: The end of the Baghdad caliphate following the Mongol invasions

1100 — 1200 — 1300 — 1400

Al-Idrisi creates the most detailed world map yet to be created

Rapid development of the hospital at Damascus

Ibn al-Nafis correctly describes the flow of blood through the heart

The astronomer of Damascus, Ibn al-Shatir, develops new models for the movements of the planets, which, in turn, influence Copernicus

Legend

West

East and West: The Conquests

Muslim Empire

Cultural and Scientific Events of the Muslim Empire

ATLANTIC
OCEAN

EUROPE

• Paris

FRANCE

SPAIN

ITALY

• Toledo

• Cordoba

GREECE

Palermo

Athens

• Ceuta

Algers

Tunis

MEDITERRANEAN SEA

Rabat

TUNISIA

ALGERIA

Tripoli

MOROCCO

LIBYA

EGY

AFRICA

MOROCCO names of countries
         in the 21st century

Toledo city

Tripoli state capital in the
         21st century

- - - - - limits of the
           Muslim Empire

The Muslim Empire in the 10th Century

RUSSIA

ARAL SEA

Uzbekistan

CASPIAN SEA

BLACK SEA

TURKEY

Bukhara

Samarkand

ASIA

Aleppo

SYRIA

Tehran

LIBYA

Damascus

IRAQ

Baghdad

Esfahan

Tigris

Euphrates

Basra

IRAN

INDIA

SAUDI ARABIA

Medina

Mecca

RED SEA

YEMEN

Sana'a

INDIAN
OCEAN